MW01048477

Dysfunctional

(The Root of Betrayal)

Tameka Oliver

AuthorHouse™
1663 Liberty Drive
Bloomington, IN 47403
www.authorhouse.com
Phone: 1-800-839-8640

First published by AuthorHouse 10/8/2010

ISBN: 978-1-4520-7348-4 (e)
ISBN: 978-1-4520-7346-0 (sc)
ISBN: 978-1-4520-7347-7 (hc)

Library of Congress Control Number: 2010913817

Printed in the United States of America

This book is printed on acid-free paper.

Allow Me To Introduce Myself

7/30/90\
Diary Entry,

Today, I turned fourteen and instead of having a pool party with my peers, I had cake and ice cream with my family members like I was FIVE again. You have got to be kidding me? First all of, how many people do you know have a party on a Monday? Jeanette, (my biological mother) figured why go through all the trouble of waiting until the weekend; I only have two friends.

The family came over and half of them could have stayed at home considering the cheap ass gifts they brought. That kiddy party was a damn disaster. That's why I sat in the corner the entire time by myself. I didn't blow out my candles, or I didn't smile for the photos- what for? How could they have expected me to be happy about an embarrassing time like this? When I opened my gifts, I frowned at most of them; tossing those dollar store items back into their gift bags. You should've seen the looks on their faces when I asked if anyone had brought the receipt with them. A few of my family members appeared angry, but not as frustrated as I was about this sorry excuse of a party. My grandmother was so mad at me, she had steam coming off of her head, but I was furious too. She sat by me, pinching me for everything that I did wrong today. I can honestly say that I have marks that will last a lifetime. Especially when I dropped a bag of ceramic puppies, my little seven-year-old cousin bought me. Oops did I do that? I didn't want that mess! I got a *hard* pinch for making her cry.

I didn't get my barbecue ribs like I asked, so I had to settle for hot dogs boiled on top of the oven, which I did not eat because my appetite was destroyed. Everyone left this stupid party mad at me. Ask me if I care…Nope, I don't. They should have known better, if they were going to do something for me; do it right! Otherwise, don't waste your time. Now my grandma knows how to do things right because she gave me money. You can't argue with money. My Uncle Charles gave me a nice gift too- a bracelet- a real diamond bracelet. The word was that he had stolen it from somewhere (oh well, it's mine now.) Jeanette gave me three diaries, beautifully wrapped in a gift box. My initial reaction was to throw those damn books, hitting her upside the head, but she was too far, and grandma already had pinched my skin off my left arm and leg. My grandma convinced me that having a diary would be a good thing. She told me that instead of always being mad and yelling at people, writing it down can relieve some steam, and might keep me from getting into so much trouble. She also said that I should consider keeping track of the good times in the book, that way I could come back and read about it. (How often do I have good times? Almost never.) She said, 'make sure you hide it because Jeanette is surely going to read it.' The type of stuff I'm probably going to put in here I'd better hide it. Oh yes, it will definitely be hidden very well.

Oh diary, allow me to introduce myself; my name is Tamara Lasha Brown. I turned 14 years old today, and I used to live with my grandma until I was eleven years old. My mother, Jeanette, fussed and complained until my grandma gave in, and I was forced to move in with *HER*. So to Jeanette's house I (sadly) went. I love music, especially Michael Jackson and Prince. I don't like to socialize with people much because they can be as phony as three-dollar bills. They pretend to care about you, and once you turn your back… STAB! Therefore, I don't give them the opportunity to get at me.

I might curse a lot, but that's the only way I know how to get my point across. Been a cursing sailor since I was seven months old (I heard,) so there's no hope of rehabilitation right now. My first word was not mama or daddy, but "Hoe."

Now, it's time for me to find a good hiding spot and take a bath. I'm long overdue for some relaxing music (The Best of George Benson) is in order to relieve me from my stressful day. Nia, (my friend) called me an ungrateful demon child, but she gets pool parties and nice gifts every year. She always has something to say about what I do, so I don't pay her comments any mind. Good night…

First Impressions

Tamara stood five feet seven inches tall. She weighed one hundred and twenty three pounds; light-complexioned, with a slender face. She owned the prettiest set of hazel-green eyes that anyone could possess, with a cute, pointy nose, and a stacked body (or so the boys at school remarked.) She wasn't built like most fourteen-year-old girls, no sir. Men often confused her for being at least twenty years old. She was a very beautiful young lady on the outside. However, on the inside, she was filled with so much animosity. She made "The Scrooge" look like a saint.

The young men at her school were intimidated by her looks and the *Rumors* surrounding her. Few of them ever spoke to her because of her evil reputation. And that was fine with her. She even preferred it that way.

In the fifth grade, a male classmate (Jordan Johnson) played a dare game and had hit her on the butt after recess- big mistake. She chased him all the way home, beating him up in front of his own home and parents. After that incident, she didn't have too many problems with the boys in her school. Then her female classmates tested her patience by spreading rumors that she liked Jason McNeal, (the boy who ate his boogers.)

She paid them back by sneaking into their lockers as they showered after gym class, stealing everyone's clothes, placing them into a big duffle bag, hiding it in the (old) abandoned janitors closet (in the basement) underneath some old used mops. She got dressed and went back to homeroom class while the locker room got turned upside down with screaming girls and panicking teachers. They questioned her on how she was the only student whom clothes were still in the locker. She replied laughing, "Whoever it was *KNEW* not to bother my damn clothes." She cackled. "You know they say that I'm crazy? Anyone could have done this because they constantly pick with people."

School Officials were unable to find the culprit responsible for the act, even though everyone had their suspicions. After that, *No One* messed with her again, nor did they ever find their clothes. And that's been three years ago.

School's out and she planned on doing her usual activities: movies, music, eating and cleaning. You couldn't tell when she was present in the home because she would be in her room as quiet as a deaf mute in a library. Whenever she *did* speak to anyone, nothing nice was being said. If you stayed out of her way, everything would be fine. She carried "two chips" on her shoulders because nothing good ever happened to her, and she didn't care about anything.

It was something different about Tamara, yes indeed. What was it about her? You sensed that something just wasn't right, and if you haven't.. (That's going to change soon….)

Present.
07-31-1990 (Tuesday)
Dear Diary,

Every day after school I have to clean up behind these two grown people. I know I'm a teenager, and I have chores to do but damn! Am I supposed to be the only one doing stuff around here? I don't think that's how it works- but hey, what can I do but raise hell? It's the summer time, so I wake up to Jeanette giving me instructions on what to do before she heads off to work, at five a.m.

"Wash the dishes; mop the floors, clean the stove off, clean out the fridge and the list goes on. She cuts into my sleep every damn morning to tell me the same stuff that I already know. I did that yesterday and the day before that right? Gosh. Damarcus, (her boyfriend) who doesn't lift a finger to pick up anything, yet, will use all ten of them to make the mess; works my last nerve.

Today, when I cleaned up the bathroom, I didn't have enough cleaning supplies to do my chores and that pissed me off, but not as much as him being downstairs laughing at me. He found my outburst and throwing of the empty container very funny. When I see Jeanette stupid self, I'm going to curse her like it's going out of style. I had to spend some of my birthday money for Ajax, so not only do I have to clean; I have to buy the stuff now.

That's great. So if it's not done by the time she gets home today, and I have to listen to her complain, I'm going to jail tonight. If she stops tagging behind him, then maybe, she could get some work done around here. She works two jobs while this bum sits around here scratching his dusty nuts and gambling with his friends. I'd rather live outside with grandma's dog than with these fools. She doesn't love me. She only wanted me here so I could take care of this house, and cook food for them. I'm her full time, personal slave, but I'm becoming more than a maid to her boyfriend. I can personally say that I understand how Cinderella must've felt. He sits in "his" recliner (the one that my aunt bought) dogging out the television set and requesting beer- after- beer (like I'm his waitress) with the remote control in one hand and a body part of mine in the other. Being in this home really tests my patience. I got to go and cook- thanks for the release valve diary. Quote for the day: "What doesn't kill you will only make you stronger." My belief, "If I don't kill you- you should be strong and leave." I will vent later.

Stepfather From Hell

Damarcus stood five feet nine- two hundred and thirty five pounds of solid tissue. He was dark complexioned with a goatee and a shiny bald, bumpy crystal ball head. He took pride in his muscle bound frame and he showed off his biceps every chance that he had. He wore shirts that were two sizes too small for him. It looked like the upper half of his body was going to explode (leaving nothing but his lower half.)

He always would find reasons to take his funny looking self-outside (especially when women were around) just to show off! He carried a bottle of baby oil in his back pocket; rubbing his arms before he would go outside was a sign that he was loony (not to mention self-centered). He was compulsively concerned with his outer image, but neglected his personal hygiene. When women were pointing and whispering, he thought they were compliments, but it was just the opposite. A little bit of soap and water never killed anyone (old spice and funk is a horrible combination.)

Tamara despised when his loud, obnoxious, dirty thug friends came over to the house to gamble. His friends messed with her because he did, and that made her irate. She became a hostage in her own home because of them. They found reasons for knocking on her door: I need some tissue... I need some soap. They wouldn't know how to use soap, if you'd wet the towel with it and gave it to them, she thought.

Last Month, their fun and games came crashing down on them. Calvin (the alcoholic out of the bunch) hemmed her against the wall, grabbing her crouch. His nuts and her left knee became acquainted, immediately followed by his right shoulder and her dinner fork that she had tucked away (for a time like this) in her back pocket. She zoomed past the gang, heading straight for her bedroom locking the door as she dialed her grandmother's number. He came from the hallway jumping up and down like a rabbit.

"Pull it out!"

"Be still," Damarcus said laughing.

"I bet that killed your buzz?" Brian added, falling down laughing.

They couldn't remove the deeply lodged fork from his shoulder because he kept moving.

"Man, you gone have to take your dumb ass to the doctor. I told you not to mess with that crazy ass girl," Damarcus said in tears, holding his side. That was the funniest sight that he had seen in a while, which didn't last long before her grandma and uncles came through the back door turning the party out. Punches were thrown, eyes were blackened, lumps were formed and feelings were hurt. The fighting ceased when the distant sound of police sirens were heard in the distance. With that, everyone began to scatter the way bugs did after the lights were turned on; some fled through the front door while others ran out the side and back doors. A few people even hopped over the fence, causing Rocky, the neighbor's Chihuahua, to run after them.

Diary Entry
08-06-1990
Dear Diary,

Today is Monday, and I hate that I had to come back to this house, but I didn't have a choice in the matter. At first, I could stay at my grandma's house for the whole summer vacation, but I heard Damarcus telling her that I was her child, and if she wanted me home that was her decision.

Today was like all the other days; cook, clean and get harassed. I literally felt sick once I got a glimpse on how messy this house was, what in the hell were they doing here? I was only gone for three days, and it looks like a tornado passed through here twice! I could slam Damarcus and Jeanette's heads together popping them off their damn bodies.

As I cleaned up today, he followed me around the house tugging on my clothes (spooning me.) Until the phone rang, he gave his undivided attention to (the mystery female) who called the house everyday around ten thirty am. I told Jeanette about his suspicious hour and a half of ***whispering*** and ***giggling*** phone session with this tramp, but she believed him over me. He told her some lame ass story. He said he was talking to his cousin on her lunch break. She's stupid, so I promised myself that I was going to have to stop him myself. He even had one of his girl cousins vouch for him. Whatever! I can't take it any longer. What are my plans for him? I have no idea, but I'm sure I will figure something out and soon.

Sooner Than Later

Tamara shifted through the house cleaning up as fast as having (*Only*) two arms allowed. Nia had taken the chance to let Tamara borrow her father's favorite movie (Godfather 3 on VHS) before he returned home from work. And she was anxious to watch the movie.

Damarcus shortened his conversation with "the mystery girl" so he could continue pestering Tamara.

"Come here," he said, drawing her closer to him.

She quickly washed out the iron skillet placing it on top of the stove as she poured the vegetable oil into it. She retrieved *"The Purple"* lighter from the drawer and lit the stove. She turned the tap down low (that it was barely lit) so she could finish cleaning and seasoning the chicken.

He smacked her across the rear end as she bent over to get a pot.

She tagged him hard across the back with the pot. "Don't do that shit, stupid!" She asked, "Did Jeanette just pull up?"

"Nah, don't even try it," he pulled her closer to him. "Come here baby."

What in the heck am I going to do? She contemplated on what to do so hard that she felt an instant migraine. If my heart beats any faster and harder, it's going to explode, she thought.

He had whispered something to her but she wasn't concentrating on his words because her nose burned from the (god awful) smell of his breath. He didn't need nose clippers (And she knew why "Gosh.")

She mustered all the strength available to get through this ordeal. He kissed and sucked on her neck (like a vampire) intensely, as she rolled her eyes to the ceiling wishing it to be over.

Now what am I going to do, she thought inside. "Are you going to force me to have sex with you again?"

"Don't try and bat those eyes at me," he explained. "You know you want this again," he said laughing.

She dry heaved at the thought, Relax, and don't throw up. Play his little game with him, she concluded. She kissed him back, unfastening the six buttons on his shirt.

"Don't peek," she whispered. She didn't know if she wanted to run to her room, out of the door, or what. "I'm going to undress for you daddy, keep them closed," she nervously looked around.

He smiled. "Undress for daddy."

The grease on the stove started to pop lightly. She kept on talking to him, but was confused on what to do next. She yelled from with, I got it!

She screamed. "Open your eyes now!"

As his eyes opened, she tossed the skillet with the hot grease in it, directly on him running up the stairs like a bolt of lightning. He had expected some hot, slippery sex, and to his surprise, he met a full skillet of hot, slippery grease. Both were hot and wet, but I couldn't fathom he would have liked the latter one instead. From afar, she heard the skillet as it hit the floor, and he yelled out in agony. His eyes had popped out of their sockets, at least that's what the glimpse that she caught, looked like before she disappeared. He screamed this high, eerie cry (that probably contacted a few aliens in another galaxy) as the grease soaked through his skin. Muscles can be penetrated too.

He charged after her (like she was a football player, he had the ball with a minute to go and his team was down by four points with five yards to go, and he had possession of the ball, and she was the end zone)- Fumble-Tamara wins.

"You fucking bitch," he yelled. "I'm going to kill you!"

She made it to her room within arm's reach of him. The closer she made it to her room, the further it seemed to be. He missed her by a nano second. He regretted that he ran after her once the pain kicked in.

"Oh my God," he yelled. He looked down at his muscular arms yelling through the hallway, "My skin is blistering up!" He kicked the door. "Open up the door, I'm not mad at you baby," he said in a guileful manner.

She lay across her bed laughing hysterically at him, as he yelled on the other side of her door.

"Get off of my door boy," she cackled. She thought back to the way he looked as she kissed him, as opposed to the way he looked as she tossed the grease. What a difference? "Woo, that was a close call," she said playfully, holding onto her stomach crying- (from laughter of course.)

"Damarcus, are you okay? Are you hot for me daddy? Do you have some new tricks to show me, huh?"

He kicked the door harder, pulling on the door handle looking like (The Incredible Hulk) instead of being green; he was pink and brown from the burns. Okay enough of the jokes, she thought. "Before he kicks my damn door down," she mumbled, as she picked up the phone to call her grandmother to come rescue her. "Hello, put grandma on the phone.

Got'cha

Damarcus' legs felt like they weighed a thousand pounds as he walked downstairs. "I'm going to kill that little tramp!"

He carefully rolled up his sleeves and inspected his arms because they were stinging terribly. He noticed blood and pus seeping through his shirt.

"What the fuck?" He stopped at the bottom of the stairs and took stock of the damage that was done to his burned body.

"Look at my chest?" he mumbled. He looked surprised as he examined the rest of his body. "Aw, man look at my chest!"

He wondered. What am I going to tell Jeanette once she gets home? Most importantly, will my chest look the same after I heal? He stood in the middle of the floor shocked at how quickly the events unfolded. I always knew that she was unstable, but I never imagined her going to this extreme. He took baby steps towards the sofa, attempting to sit down, but not realizing that the pain was going to be too much to bear.

"Fuck!"

The street was filled with smoke from William and Jay burning rubber (like fools) en route to Jeanette's house. All you heard was the sound of William's car-back firing from time to time as they rode down Dickerson Street in complete silence. The ride to the house was a brief, but humid trip because his car windows weren't working (Uncle William claimed that it was because the fuse had blown; if that's the problem, Tamara wondered, then why not replace it? It's just raggedy.) They were mad--and now uncontrollably miserable from the summer heat, it made matters worse. They boiled on the inside and outside.

Barbara sat hunched down in the seat counting the trees as he drove past (relaxing her nerves, keeping her mind off the heat and Damarcus.)

Once they arrived around the corner from the house, Barbara had hopped out of the car before William had a chance to park it.

"Will you hide that bat please?" William asked. "You can't walk down the street with that thing out in the open like that Barb!" he said laughing. She guiltily glanced up and down the block to make sure that no one had seen her going into the trunk to retrieve William's leather jacket. What is she doing? Jay wondered as he watched his sister tuck the bat underneath the jacket.

"Come on, let's go," she commanded. "We are wasting time," Barbara made them aware of this fact as they walked down the street looking like a group of Wild West Outlaws. (All they needed were matching cowboy hats, boots and guns.) Barbara was mildly surprised to discover that no one was outside, and that was a good sign, however unusual for a summer night.

Barbara stood five foot-two (the shortest in the pack) with long straight, jet-black hair (that was in a ponytail today) with a round, apple shaped face. Nothing about her vibe made you feel threatened, but baby- she turned into a beast when you messed with her children. She said it was something that lurked deep within her, but came out when there was a need. Being the oldest sibling of ten, you almost *had* to develop that protective trait. You simply *had* to.

Damarcus made a conscious effort not to let his legs rub because it sent chills up his spine. He carefully removed his pinkish, pus and blood-stained shirt tossing it onto the floor, pressing his lips together to avoid making wimpy sounds. He didn't know what to do because even though he didn't feel like standing, he was sure as hell not going to sit down. His body felt like it had been burned alive (which it actually had with grease) so he decided to clean the wounds to see how bad they really were. He walked with his legs spread apart looking like the boogeyman and headed to the bathroom's cabinet.

He took hold of the pile of Tamara's favorite towels from the cabinet and the jar of Vaseline, which his mother swore was the cure-all for any type of wound…gunshots; use Vaseline. I fell off my bike, and there's a big hole in my arm (clean it and use Vaseline.) I smashed my hand in the car, and I think it's broke (get some ice, and bring the Vaseline.)

Sure enough; he picked up the phone, and asked his mother what was good for burns, and you guessed it, she said butter and Vaseline. "Just making sure ma," he said, giggling a little.

"Who's hurt Marcus?"

"Brian burned his hand while cooking chicken," he lied.

"Oh yeah," she said matter of factly. "Tell him to run cold water on his hand, spread the butter on the burn first, and then put the Vaseline on it. What was he doing trying to cook?"

"I don't know ma, I'll talk to you later, okay?"

"I love you son," she said to him. He forced a smile and replied, "Same here ma."

As he looked into the mirror, he became upset. He pictured his boys teasing him for what he had allowed Tamara to do to him. It wasn't that long ago that he stood in his kitchen laughing at Calvin with the fork stuck into his shoulder. Calvin would have pissed his pants from laughter if he had known Damarcus' current predicament.

"Ladies and gentlemen, I now would like to bring to the stage our very own, "Third-Degree-Burn-Victim!" (The crowd goes wild.) "Here's Damarcus!"

He cautiously cleaned the burns with a cold towel, as many as he could handle without literally crying. Forty percent of his left side, from his head to his feet, had burned and was now full of blisters.

'You better go to the doctor,' he envisioned his friend Donald laughing at him saying. 'I can't believe you and Calvin let that little bitch do that to y'all?'

He thought. You got my friends laughing at me. Damarcus pictured going upstairs, breaking down her door and strangling her until her hazel eyes bulged out of their sockets.

He heard the front door open, and he thought, that's Jeanette, what am I going to tell her? I'll figure something out. The door slammed. He said, as he walked toward the living room, "Hey, guess what Tamara did? Baby, she-"

William asked, "No baby, what did she do? He swung the bat, knocking him unconscious.

"What's going on?" he asked after he had regained consciousness. His head throbbed, his vision was blurred, and his wrists were hurting because the rope was tied extra tight behind the chair. Barbara awakened him by splashing ice cold water from the fridge on him.

"Get yo ass up!" Charles yelled, smacking him in the face. His girlfriend's family stood in a circle (like a cult) taking turns smashing his already sore, burned body.

"We got'cha n***a," Jay smirked. "You touched my motherfucking niece?

08/10/90 Friday

Dear Diary,

I'm back at my grandmother's house where I want to be. The ride from my house to grandma's house required five point six extended miles and thirty extra minutes. I tossed the keys down from my bedroom to grandma, and they came into the house to get me, but they were more interested in getting Damarcus. My grandmother wanted me to go out to my uncle's car and wait until they were done, but I wasn't going to miss out on a two- year plan as it unfolded. I'll explain it to you. I never liked Damarcus from the moment that I laid eyes on him, once he moved in, the plotting began. I told Jeanette about him touching on me (I was lying at the time, but he soon did start) and like always she believed him. I knew with a little inspiration, (me wearing booty shorts and tight baby doll shirts) he would have fallen victim. Sleeping with him was the worst thing that I had to endure for revenge, so I would either give in, or he probably would have taken it. I purposely left behind condom packages in Jeanette's drawers so she could see them. He would say, "It wasn't me, ask Tamara. Maybe she was in here with someone." I went as far as leaving my panties underneath her side of the bed for her to notice, and nothing was said from her. "He's raping me, I would say to her," and she replied. "Why are you trying so hard to break us up?" I could break her in half, with her skinny, trifling self. Maybe, he wasn't raping me but he sure was knocking boots with me from time and time. Anyway, I peeped around the corner as they (Lexis, Lynette, Grandma and her three brothers) "literally" beat the crap out of him. They tied him to our dining room chair as they questioned him, striking him with every stupid response. He made the mistake of trying to fight back. He attempted to ram his head into Uncle Charles' stomach but Charles dodged his attempt and Burn Victim's head was introduced to the thick glass table. Damarcus slumped to the floor.

"Oh, this dumb ass ni**a den killed himself," Charles said laughing. Everyone stood there looking crazy because they had no plans of discarding a dead body. Barbara checked for a pulse, and there wasn't one.

"Oh shit," she thought. They cleaned up the house so they wouldn't leave any evidence behind. Without being seen, they removed his body from the house. Jay wrapped his body up in carpet and plastic, drove the truck to the door and (Will and Charles) carried him out, playing it off like they had installed carpet in the house. Good thing he owned a carpet business because the truck came in handy. Their actions didn't look too suspicious. It took over three hours to get everything situated before they took him to his final resting place. They made us (Lynette, Alexis and I) wear our shirts over our faces so we couldn't see where they were taking him, not knowing that I could see right through my T-shirt. I just wanted to be nosey and see where they were taking him- Northeastern High School. The school had burned some years back, and so they carried him in, and left him there to rot. It was a deserted part of the city; no homes were in the area (it was the perfect place.) I could tell that my grandmother didn't feel good about what had happened, but my uncles could care less. They didn't like him from the way he beat on Jeanette some years back. I knew that my grandma would come and get me from that hell-hole. I know that I will probably have to go back with Jeanette, but at least he won't be here. If my daddy isn't there with me, no man will be living in the house with us. I'm "fatherless" so she will be "man less," until I'm grown. She wants me here so she must deal with my atrocious ways. This was retaliation because she didn't believe me; she didn't put her blood first. I thought that blood was thicker than water, but I guess Jeanette didn't get that memo. Let's see how she's going to act since her beloved king is gone.

Diary Entry 3
08/12/90 (Sunday)
Dear Diary,

This entry today will cover a lot of information that I've learned over the time spent at my grandmother's house. You know when you are little and when older people start talking about juicy stuff. You either have to go outside and play, or go into another part of the house that was far, far away from them. Grown folks' business is what they call it. I've heard some horror stories of what happened to kids who didn't move when they said so. Those caught lingering around with their ears pinned back; got tobacco spat into their faces, or pinched until the white meat on their arms showed- (abuse, I call it.) After we got to my grandmother's house from dropping Damarcus off that night, we sat at the table talking. Not about what had happened because we made a vow to never discuss what happened EVER again to ANYONE, not even amongst each other. This was the first time that I could sit in on "The Grown Folks Session," I felt like a member of a secret society. Now, I must admit, I would have probably received tobacco in my face, and my arms might've been permanently white because eavesdropping should've been my middle name. I know a lot of what's going on around here but there's a lot that I didn't know either, and that day, I learned so much more. Black History Month came early for me this year. I never understood who picked February (the shortest month of the year- what a slap in the face.) I was getting my lesson, and I wasn't learning about the same old people; Martin Luther King, Rosa Parks, Sojourner Truth and Malcolm X- not bashing them in any way, but in class, it was a repeat of the same people. I knew each of their lives probably better than their children. I always did research on different people for my projects. The meaning of this month was to learn new, exciting things about Black People. I would have my teacher's undivided attention in History class as I would recite my essays- she would tell me, "Aaah that was very interesting I never knew Charles Drew invented that!"

"I guess not- because you didn't care. I know that I write so many different things to you from time to time." I hope that I have explained myself well enough so that you don't get lost, and I know it can be confusing. I have so many weird family members and we, as a family, go through a lot of challenging issues, and I'm not to blame for all of them (well, maybe a few.) And if I can take this time to explain a little about some of them, you won't be so lost later. This would be like a history lesson of my family. You can always use this as a reference guide if you don't know who I'm referring to. Breaking news bits about my family are as frequent as tornadoes in Kansas. It might be boring like class, but like I have learned everything; even those that might be dreadful to listen to may have a purpose. Here goes nothing… Barbara Ann Jones, my grandmother, raised me from birth to eleven years old. She's sweet as pie, but like pies, they are appealing to the eye, can be nice and tasty to some, but if kept in the oven, can get nasty if you make her. I love her dearly. Rumor has it that she was a piece of work when raising her children, along with my grandfather, William Earl Brown. They created four children out of this twenty five year marriage; my mother Jeanette, my Aunt Diane who's the family's book worm and activist of everything, my other Aunt Alexis (my sworn enemy, who I believe was born to be a thorn in my side) and finally Auntie Nette who acts like a baby (she plays games all day and never does what she is told. She never takes anything serious, everything is humorous, and I could knock her big head off.) My grandfather died two years ago from a heart attack, and that sent a shockwave throughout the entire family. My grandfather had eight siblings, and they each had at least five children. We need two Belle Isle sized parks for them alone. I don't even know half of their names, so I can't write about something that I don't know. Sorry. My grandmother has eight siblings, but I know this side all too well: Jason, the second oldest died when he was thirty from a car accident and left behind his two children Javon and Gavin for grandma to care for. The boys' mother died from complications after giving birth. Charles was the third oldest, and con-artist of the century. William, granddaddy's twin, who attempts to be on the straight and narrow, but gets drawn into bullshit because of his family. Jay; the ghetto businessman who loves to boast on his job and his many dames (who thinks that because his name is on the side of a truck, and that he has professional looking business cards, that he can get any woman to just drop their panties. He's "***The Man***," Oh please! He sells and installs carpets for a living, for crying out loud. Her sisters are; Ann, who has five kids of her own- too many to name, Louise, the Wicked Witch of the East, (no explanation necessary) with four of the most horrendous acting kids that ever walked this earth; Max, (who's never around the family, she does her own thing) and baby sister Sandy, who teaches at Ferry Elementary School. Grandma went to cosmetology school when she arrived in Michigan, but has been doing her sisters' hair since she was ten. She became Alabama's youngest beautician and that's how I came to be. My grandmother had a customer, they called her Dee, she paid my grandma to do her hair, and that's how Jeanette and Trent met, while grandma and Dee mixed up perm and shared recipes. Their children were under the stairs, or in the shed sharing and mixing body fluids. Trent's family had money and so when they found out that Jeanette was pregnant, they didn't want to have any part of that child whether if it was his or not. See my father was tied up with this other girl whose parents had money, so they wanted to associate only with their "kind." Sure grandma was good enough to do her hair; that was a service she needed; Dee thought that she was better than us. After I was born, horns came through skulls, blood was shed and bones were fractured. It was something else grandma explained to me; a family war that would've made the ***Hatfields*** and ***McCoys*** seem like the Peace Corps. Eventually, someone was going to die. Grandma went to jail for breaking windows out of Dee's house trying to fight her, but that was only after Dee told

Jeanette not to send any more letters or pictures of "that" baby to her house because she wasn't her grandchild. "Oh wow, Grandmother." They ended up moving to Detroit after granddaddy got a job at Ford Motor Company, but not before people took trips to the hospital (both sides.) Now that brings us to our current set of problems; Jeanette walks around looking pitiful and heavyhearted because Damarcus hasn't called or came home. She's so sad, all she does is eat and lie down. Juan and Alexis are an item and have been for quite some time now. Grandma doesn't like him much, but she's twenty- two, so she's in that rebellious phase. This short, peanut headed boy thinks he's God's gift to women, and I don't see why because he's not attractive at all… (Well, not to me at least.) I watch them when they are around, and I think he's a punk. You know how some men have a kind of "protective vibe" about them? Like if you were in danger, you didn't have any uncertainty that he would stand up and fight for you, or at least with you…Well, I'm sorry to report that Juan looks like the type of person that would sacrifice your ass so he could get away. (Scooby Doo would fight before he would and we all know about old Scooby.) He always looks petrified and apprehensive about something. Jerry, Lynette's boyfriend, (who's an overweight comedian) strives for attention and makes jokes about people, when he looks like he's one burger shy of explosion. Where in the hell did she find Jerry? Actually, where in the hell did they find these jerks? Excuse me miss? Can you point me in the direction where I can return these men? Wishing it was that simple.☺

Diane's previous love interests consisted of books, homework and more books. Can you say revenge of the nerds? She's the darkest one in the gang, and I think she's dealing with issues since everyone else is light skinned or brown. As far as looks go, we all bear a resemblance of each other, and you can sure tell that we are family, even Darkie. She's going through something because she has "gone" and completely changed her apparel. "Gone," are the unappealing overalls, replaced by denim jeans, and her bi-focal glasses have been swapped out in favor of colored contacts. Perhaps it's this new "mystery" guy she's been seeing who's responsible for this transformation—whatever the reason, it's good to see her happy at least. Nia, my best-friend, (well that's what she calls herself) resides around the corner from my grandmother, and I'm kind of involved with her brother, Charles, I used to be in love with him, but he never looked at me twice because of Adrian Chattel, so once I came back to grandma's house this past summer, (he probably just realized my C cups and my fuller jeans) he's interested, and now I'm not, but I talk to him just to conquer something that I always wished for. Okay, I've explained a lot about my family to you, so you shouldn't be confused when I tell you a story, dear diary. It's eight o' clock, and the Cosby's are on…Good night.

Tamara

Back Down Memory Lane

"Let's Get It On," played softly in the background on the kitchen's small radio as Jeanette and her mother had one of those, "Grown Folk" conferences going on at a moderate, peaceful, tone. Jeanette took a seat at the far end of the table sipping on some tea while her mother washed the dishes. Alexis moved like a zombie from her room to the bathroom, and back without noticing anyone was in the kitchen. Javon and Gavin had left the house around ten this morning to handle their regular drug dealings. Tamara searched for a secret place to hide her diary for when she visited on the weekends. "I can't put it here," she said, as she had attempted to put it behind the dresser. Every place she thought of wasn't good enough because it was accessible. In the back of Tamara's closet, there was a small door that had a piece of wood that nailed it shut.

"What do we have here?" With great force she removed the piece of wood from the wall with a hammer that she kept underneath her mattress and opened the secret door. She retrieved her flashlight from under her pillow and checked out the storage space. She'd tucked the book up against the wall and used the wood to cover it up. "Look at all these damn spiders," she said, holding her hand over her mouth. "I hope I don't come across one, or a dead corpse in here," she nervously looked in. She thought that she heard voices in the kitchen, so she decided to go out there and be nosey. Barbara and Jeanette looked like they were having a serious conversation so Tamara tiptoed to the sofa and listened in.

"She's my child mama, and I know her," Jeanette mumbled.

"I'm not disputing that she's your child, but I know her as well, I did raise her for the first eleven years of her life," Barbara mentioned. "You've only had her for three years now."

She laughed softly. "Maybe so, but these are the worst years -her teenage years. She-"

Barbara interrupted. "I'll take her back, she can't be any worse than you and your sisters during y'all terrible teenage years."

"Hmm," Jeanette chuckled. "I wasn't that bad and you know it mama," she said giggling.

"You got mad at me and left home because I told you not to write or try to contact Trent. You blamed me because Dee didn't want you and Trent to be together. I went to jail over the situation an-"

"Mama, you only made matters worse," she retorted. "We were going to work things out, Trent and I. And I asked you not to keep the confusion brewing, but you didn't listen to me."

(Jeanette and Barbara could be together laughing and hugging, but when this topic was brought up, cursing and door slamming soon followed, and today it most likely would end on the same note.)

"Are you stuck on stupid Jeanette? Or you are just plain retarded?" She shook her head out of pure disgust. "If you didn't see that I was doing what was best for you and the baby. Then, I really don't know what to tell you," she said, slamming her cup down on the table. (And the slamming begins.) "No matter what you said that boy wasn't going to go against "his mother" for you or anyone else. They had money, so she turned her nose up and frowned down on us. She only had money from her inheritance other than that she would have been like the rest of us!"

"But-"

"But, my ass," Barbara screamed. (There's the cursing.) "Once you "become" a mother you will understand that you don't allow people to mistreat your children and still let them interact with them. She said the baby wasn't his, and so you got mad when you had to get an abortion. They weren't going to help take care of the baby, and they made that very clear. We were barely making ends meet, living check to check. So I didn't know where to turn. And then a month later you turned around and got pregnant again by him and hid it from me," shaking her head. "But you got mad at me! He used you because he had no business sleeping with you! He had a fiancée, so Dee had to cover his shit up. She wasn't going to let your- what did she call you, let me think," she looked up at the ceiling. "Your low-life, slutty, ass ruin his life."

"She w-"

Barbara swung her hand up to intercept. "I went to jail, and my brother was put in the hospital from her brothers beating him up. Your father and uncle lost their jobs because of this. All of them were put in jail from fighting at that bar and ended up with many cuts and broken bones. Your so-called friends turned their backs on you, but the final straw was when they tossed a cocktail bomb in our stables. It was just a matter of time before someone died."

"I didn't ask any of you to fight over that! Y'all like to fight!"

Barbara ignored Jeanette and massaged her temples to relieve her migraine. "One, two, three," she exhaled and counted.

"I didn't come here to talk about that Mama, that's water under the bridge," she said. "I came to see if Tamara wanted to come home early, or if she wanted to stay a few more days. You were the one who told me to get out of the car. I wasn't even going to come in."

Barbara marched over to the counter, and poured herself a second cup of coffee. "Speaking of Tamara- I need to talk to you about her?"

She exhaled. "What about her? What did she do now," Jeanette wondered aloud.

"You want some more tea?" Barbara rose from the table, but Jeanette declined on the tea. She cleared her throat pondering on how to come out and tell her. "Friday, Tamara called me crying saying that Damarcus had tried to rape her, so we had to go to the house and get her-"

"What? Mama, I'm so tired of Tamara's fabricated stories. We've went over this before, and I'm sick to death of it!" Jeanette struck the table with her hand and scooted away from the table.

"What makes you so sure that she's lying? Barbara asked. "Or are you just hoping that she is? Besides, I believe her because she has no reason to lie on him," she coughed. "I don't see why you allowed an ex-convict to move in with you and your daughter."

She chuckled. "You always tried to regulate everything that your children did, and I despised that. I know him, and he didn't lay a hand on her, she doesn't like him, and none of y'all do either!"

Barbara experienced the stiffness in her shoulders so she decided to move away from Jeanette before she struck her for talking senseless. She washed her cup out and wiped down the counter for the *THIRD* consecutive time. "You work all day and you got her there with him and his friends. I guess you didn't take heed when Calvin tried to touch her, or she was lying about that too?"

Jeanette rose up from the table. "If you believed he raped her, why didn't anyone take her to the hospital, or call the police?"

"How do you know that we didn't take her, or never made a report to the police?"

"Did you?"

Barbara chuckled. "You mean to tell me that you didn't expect for something like this to happen with all those strange men around? No one said you should not have been with him, but living with y'all should have been a no-no. What about him pounding on you? Love isn't supposed to hurt baby."

"No one is perfect--you remained with daddy after you found out about him and Aunt Max--" Barbara had whacked her across the face before she could finish. "How dare you try and throw that up in my face like that, and how dare you speak about your father like that? He's been nothing but good to you girls!"

"And he was good to Aunt Max too, I heard!" she replied sarcastically, holding her left cheek. "You forgave daddy, but never spoke to your sister again."

Barbara temporarily lost control once she stood in front of Jeanette's disrespectful mouth reaching for the collar of her shirt to choke the life out of her, but Jeanette quickly moved to the other side of the table. "I don't have to stand here and take this, I'm grown," she said.

Tamara walked in laughing. "What in the world is going on in here? World War III?" she asked, stepping in between them as Barbara was telling Jeanette that she wouldn't know how to be grown if it jumped in her ass and took over her body. "You know, just because you work doesn't make you grown. Tamara does all the work around the house so you can shut up using the word GROWN. An adult would have raised their own child, not been in the streets with every Tom, Dick and Harry! A grown person would not willingly put their child in harm's way for a piece of sorry dick!"

"Okay, okay...Look, Jeanette, I think you should leave," Alexis, said. "Mama's eyebrows are starting to connect, so you know after that I won't be able to save you, so come on."

"Get your hands off of me!" Jeanette yelled as she snatched away from Alexis.

"I'll leave when *I* get ready to leave! This isn't your house-"

"But you're upsetting my damn mama, so you should leave. You manage to do this shit every time you come round here. Just leave Nette!"

Jeanette looked at Tamara. "So...uh--are you going home or what?"

"You don't have to go if you don't want! Let her ass stay in that house with that crazy man!"

Alexis gently pushed her mother into the living room on the couch before she had raised her pressure too high. The veins in her forehead had become visible.

"Mama calm down. That IS her daughter, remember?"

"I don't give a shit," she stated.

"I'm not ready to go to your house. You and Damarcus don't want me there anyway," came from the kitchen.

Oh they about to start, Alexis thought. "I don't feel like being a mediator today, damn."

The Confrontation

Juan cruised down Alexis's street to see if her room light was on; it wasn't. He parked at the end of the block and walked down to the house. He watched over his shoulders making sure that no one trailed him. A reoccurrence of last's month robbery was not in his plans. "A few more houses," he told himself.

It was three fifty in the morning and Lexis would most likely be dead to the world, but it was imperative that he talked to her. Their phone conversation earlier didn't end on a good note and he wanted to straighten some problems out.

He pondered. Please let Alexis be in her room alone, and up, he'd crossed his fingers praying to himself, as he lightly tapped on her bedroom window. He paused a few seconds before he sought for something to stand on. He discovered a brick lying nearby the bushes; he positioned it by the window, so he could look through her window. He decided that if she didn't soon approach, he was going to run off.

Alexis had become aware of a shadow and figured that it was Juan. She eased out of her bed tiptoeing out of the house and around the back to the side.

"Boo," she yelled, nudging him in the back causing him to stumble off the brick.

His eyes were bulged and frightened. "Girl, are you crazy?" He said as he held his fast pulsating heart. "Why did you do that?"

She giggled. "You are such a scary cat Juan," she said, holding her stomach. "You thought that I was my mama?"

"I didn't know who you were. Don't do that again," he retorted.

She asked him why he came over so late, and what did he want with her.

"You hung up on me, so I decided to come by," he explained to her.

She tilted her body toward the streetlight and looked at her watch. "That was what- three hours ago so you weren't that concerned about me being mad at you."

He stood there all childlike fumbling with his fingers. Something he had a tendency of doing when he was lying to you. "I had some important runs to make, but after I took care of that I came straight over here to see you," he said, trying to lure her close to him."

"You should have kept on past here because I don't believe you," she said, as she snatched away from him.

"Why did you hang up on me?" he whispered in her ear.

She shook her head. "I didn't have time to argue with you about keeping my baby, and I'm not about to argue with you about it," she folded her arms.

"That's why you are here now –to talk about that? It's my baby- my body and I haven't decided what I want to do yet, and you will not convince me, one way or the other."

She started towards the front of the house, and he followed. She continued fussing at him, almost like his mother had done now and again, but his mind was someplace else- somewhere far away.

Should I tell her, he contemplated.

He started biting his nails another one of his habits he did when he was either lying or was deep in thought- at this split second he was doing a little of both. "I have something to tell you."

"What is it?"

"I have two kids already- ages three and five; both are girls. Their mother lives in Flint with her mother."

"WHAT?" She felt a sick, dropping sensation in her abdomen like never before. Not coming close to the way that she felt in the morning when she vomited up her food.

He held his head down fumbling with his fingers again. "No, I'm serious."

For one exceedingly, weird second Juan's jaws moved, but she didn't make out a word that had come through. "How come that wasn't a factor in the matter before this had happened, and when were you going to tell me about your other family?"

He didn't like the way that she had said "other family" as to say that she was keeping the baby. He didn't have a family, not his children and damn sure not the people he called his parents.

Juan carried around a big, dark secret that plagued him every single day no matter how hard he struggled to forget about it. His upbringing was difficult from the tender age of three until he moved with his mother's sister Beverly at the age of twelve.

His father had thrown him into the cold, creepy basement, whenever he felt he'd misbehaved. How was it being mischievous to ask for another tuna sandwich if you were still starving? The older that he became, his father created motives to lock him down the basement until the next day, or sometimes even for days. He spent a week in the underground room once for sprinting away from his father as he tried to beat him for turning on the television, although no one was watching it. His father was infuriated because he had been out-smarted, and if it weren't for that dog's ***stupid*** chewing toy, he would've escaped and wasn't going back. The damn dog received better treatment than him and his mother. Brutis (the huge Rockweiler) slept in the cold basement, but he was given a comforter to lie on at least- no cover was given to Juan.

In the winter months, he had to take the (hairy, smelly) cover from the dog to sleep underneath it. Brutis ate at least twice a day, and they screamed bloody murder if he asked to eat once a day. The dog was allowed to go outside and had toys to play with once he came inside but it was to school and back for Juan and toys were out of the question. (His toys were too expensive his father claimed.)

As many nights as he stayed in the basement he had never become accustomed to it. He was every bit as petrified of basements *now* as much as he had been when he was younger. He was especially terrified of the furnace because it made a horrible sound that intimidated him still. The clothes that hung on the clothesline looked as though people were dancing- from the air that blew out of the vent. He was pretty sure that he'd seen ghosts as he tried to sleep, and the abrupt barking from Brutis didn't help matters.

After the abuse was over, his father told him that he was trying to make a man out of him, but he'd managed to do quite the opposite. His mother wailed, fussing at him time after time. "You should not do anything wrong around Richard." Breathing was wrong to Richard. He imagined her saying to him. "I tried to warn you, but you're so hard headed. I told you not to touch anything in here."

That was the day that he realized that his mother didn't like what his father was doing, but she was helpless to do anything to stop it, so he decided that he was going to get out for good. His mother always told him, "If somebody is doing something to you that you don't like tell a schoolteacher, or another grown person and he or she will help you."

Until today, he never paid attention to his mother's long-forgotten advice. He remembered when he was five and heard those words from her, and that she had a sister named Beverly, who lived in Michigan. They lived in Atlanta. The last time he had seen his mother, she had kissed him and told him that she'd loved him regardless of what he assumed. It was like she had known that she wasn't going to see her only son again.

His aunt took him in after Juan told his gym teacher what his father was doing to him, and how his mother allowed it. The court of law immediately stepped in and removed him from the abusive home with his parents. Living with his aunt wasn't so terrible; she was never at home because she lived her life as a call girl, which she called working for an escort service. (If that helped her sleep better at night; on the nights that she had actually come back home.) He didn't mind being left alone, as long as he wasn't confined to the basement and could eat as much food as his belly could hold.

His father croaked last month from lung cancer. He didn't feel remorseful, and he sure as hell didn't attend the funeral. When he'd heard the news, he felt a sudden tinge of resentment, followed by a quick feeling of guilt because he had known that wasn't right.

"Juan, are you listening to me," Alexis asked, snapping her fingers in front of his face. "Juan!"

"I didn't tell you because my business is my business," he replied. "Who I was going with and how many kids that I have didn't affect us. I didn't think you were going to get pregnant."

She said aggravated, "I told you to put on another condom, but no, you said you knew what you were doing! Did you think I was sterile?"

"I know what I am doing."

"We wouldn't be here discussing this if that were true." She asked, "What kind of father are you to those kids, you never visit them? You are either on the block slanging them drugs, or over to my house."

"You don't know what the fuck I do when I'm not with you. I'm only around you because you asked me to be-"

She interrupted. "You live a normal life while the mother struggles to take care of the kids."

He exhaled. "Will you get off of that? I didn't tell her to have those damn kids- just like I'm trying to express you, I don't want any kids! If you have it- you are on your own," he stuffed ninety dollars in her shirt and started walking away.

"Don't you walk away from me! You stupid, abrasive, foolish, ignorant, self-centered, obnoxious, irresponsible, pompous ass! You are a sorry excuse of a man!"

He gazed at her with a devilish grin on his face not showing concern for her, or *the situation*. "Look, do what you want to do. I gotta go," he said sarcastically, gently moving her aside as he walked up the street.

She'd cursed him until he was clear out of sight. Barbara and her ***favorite bat*** (Fracture Craniums) peeped out of the front window anxiously waiting on him to bust- a- move. One yank of an arm or any hostile movement would've earned him a one way ticket to the Emergency Room. He had left so she tipped toed through the house, creeping back into her dark bedroom like a thief in the night. Another day, another problem, she thought.

Alexis sat on the porch bawling uncontrollably with her head on her lap until the sound of someone walking through the house garnered her attention.

"What are you doing out here?" Lynette questioned.

Alexis quickly rose from the porch and brushed past Lynette and headed for her room. She locked the door and cried herself to sleep as she thought about what Juan had said. His words cut deeper than a knife.

My Decision

"Not again," Lexis mumbled to herself as her mouth filled with saliva. She shut her eyes and took in deep breaths, turning onto her side. She anticipated that would've made the feeling go away but it didn't. She shielded her mouth, jumped out of bed and headed straight for the bathroom. Unfortunately, her pajamas and the floor caught most of her breakfast. She didn't like the fact that she lost total control of her bodily functions after she ate. I haven't peed on myself since I was two years old she shook her head thinking. She supposed that vomiting should have made her feel better, but it hadn't; not a second of alleviation. I was misinformed by my doctor. He said that I was experiencing morning sickness, yet, I've experienced this feeling all day and all night, sleep is my only escape. It's Morning Sickness my ass. I promise I won't put myself through this again. It's horrible, she told herself.

Barbara heard Alexis vomiting through the bathroom's vent. She stopped washing clothes and had gone upstairs to check on her. She knocked on the door to make sure that she was all right, (as if there was anything that she could have done.) She muttered that she was okay, wiping her mouth as she commenced to brush her teeth. She tried stopping the urge to vomit as she brushed her teeth like she had done a million times before, but now it became a challenge. This feeling was awful. She felt lightheaded again, so she quickly showered before Diane came to take her to the clinic. Diane was never late for anything; she didn't operate on C.P Time. After she stepped out of the shower, she hurried into her room to stretch across the bed because lying down eased her queasiness.

She gawked at the ceiling as she intently looked into L.L Cool J's eyes (a poster of course,) asking him (like he was going to respond,) if she was going to be all right after the procedure. She had her room painted his favorite color (red), and the walls were plastered with images of him everywhere. She was smitten with him ever since she heard "*I Need Love*."

She apprehensively watched the minutes on the alarm clock tick closer to nine o' clock. One thing that she couldn't wait to end was the constant arguing with her mother about getting the procedure done, and being sick from eating and certain smells. Furthermore, Juan not wanting the baby hadn't helped the situation out either.

Barbara wandered into her room and sat on the corner of the bed explaining to Alexis' that they didn't need Juan, his aunt's money or their support. She had traveled down this road before with Jeanette years ago, and she wasn't about to make the same mistake twice. Barbara tried to convey what she had heard about the procedure, but she'd managed to make it sound nothing less than "tormenting."

Diane knocked on the bedroom door, bursting in. "Are you ready?"

"Damn, why do you bother to knock if you're just going to burst in?" she asked. "Yes, I'm ready," but her brain thought a different way.

Barbara realized that their discussion hadn't changed her daughter's mind. She had made her decision. She *was* going to go through with it. She cleaned the house from top to bottom whenever she was worried about something. At this precise moment, she frantically wiped down the walls in the living room, as she babbled to herself. Alexis knew that she wasn't going to be able to get out of the house without one last appeal from her mother. And she was right.

"You don't have to do this Lexis," she said, still wiping the base of the windows.

"Mama, I don't feel like this today," she said. "I'm too young for a baby right now."

"You should've thought about that before you got yourself into this situation, besides, I told you that boy was no good!"

She exhaled. "That's irrelevant now mama, I have found that out the hard way and on my own."

She shook her head. "You girls never listen to me, and you're still not listening," she rotated to Diane. "I'm surprised that you allowed her to put you in the middle of this."

Oh boy, Diane thought. "You've taught us to stick together no matter what, and because she is doing something that you oppose mama, you are angry. I don't think that is fair ma. This is her decision and I'm supporting whatever she decides to do," Diane said as she walked towards the door. "Bye mama, I love you old lady," she said laughing.

"Bye ma," Alexis said.

"Hmm," she replied. Barbara despised when Diane had persuasive facts about things, and she couldn't argue with them. *No one asked her to be right today, she thought.*

Jeanette and Barbara's relationship hasn't been the same since that hot day in August 1975, when they took that trip to see Dr. Brooks for an abortion. Even though she tried stopping Alexis from going through with it, she just wanted to fight on the behalf of her unborn grandchild. He or she can't talk so I tried to do it for the baby. She took a break from cleaning long enough to get onto her knees and say a prayer- I tried- "It's in your hands now Lord."

Drama Queens

Marion had unloaded the girls off at Eastland Mall, and they walked in and out after he had vanished from the parking lot.

"How do you know that he's gone," Lexis asked.

She giggled. "He just left, and I'll bet, he's already past Crusade Street."

They were in store for a forty-minute hike from the mall to the clinic. They reminisced about the different occasions that their mother had shown out on them, or on other people making the long walk not too bad. Diane complained about how many liquor stores that she had counted on the way to the mall.

"Seven stores, I tell you- that's too many!"

She's about to start- oh Jesus help, Alexis prayed. She said laughing, "You nitpick about everything; everything is a conspiracy to you. Please don't embarrass me in here?"

"Embarrass you?" she snickered. "You got me going into a clinic where I don't want to go and don't feel-"

Alexis grabbed her sister's arm hauling her off of Eight Mile's busy intersection one-way; as they ran to the inside lane once the coast was clear. They leaped right out of the frying pan straight into the skillet making it to the other side of the street. Sharks were anticipating their arrival.

A little old, white woman and two men were posted like soldiers in front of the private clinic. They badgered the patients as they approached the corners of the clinic from both directions. Alexis understood why they felt they needed to be there, but she wasn't feeling well, and her mind was made up. She didn't want to hear what anyone had to say.

The frail old lady pushed around a stroller with a picture of a dead fetus on a poster board, looking to make eye contact with you, so she could begin her ritual of salvation. These pro-life crusaders reminded Diane of the beggars she would encounter at the neighborhood stores, as long as you didn't make eye contact with them, they usually wouldn't ask you for "spare" change. She tried to look "busy" and avoid looking at the old lady as she walked towards the entrance of the clinic. The man at the opposite corner was talking and passing out Rosaries and praying for people. Alexis disregarded them all walking ahead, but the woman's eyes trapped Diane's and she turned the poster board around so that Diane could see AND hear what she had to say, but the conversation took a funny turn. She had stopped the wrong person today.

"First of all, what makes you assume that I'm even pregnant?" she asked. "You heard that saying about ASSUMING? You obviously have every right to walk up and down this street, but harassing people isn't cool. This clinic provides pregnancy tests and ultrasounds so you don't know why people are here, and I feel it's an invasion of their privacy, nonetheless. How would you feel if we came to your job boycotting that your company is destroying the ozone layer, and you should quit?"

"Diane Nicole Brown! Come on," she roared.

The woman and a few (nosey) clients stood there stunned listening to her get them straight. As they walked into the room it fell silent (you heard the people breathing.) Alexis rolled her eyes as she walked toward the sign in sheet. Diane's nose burned instantly from the strong smell of rubbing alcohol. The setting reminded her of the urgent care that she had gone to when she fell off her bike requiring stitches.

The clinic was packed like a can or sardines. Inside sat thirteen teenagers: five black girls, seven white girls and one Hispanic girl, who sat next to their boyfriends, mother or friend, and now its six black girls and her sister. The door creaked.

"Jessica Taylor."

She looked like a sad puppy when she asked her mother to go in the back with her because she was scared. Her mother declined. She said since she wasn't there when she'd gotten pregnant, she wasn't going to be back there when she terminated it. "You're on your own big girl- no time to be scared now. I told you," was all that she said sarcastically.

Her daughter stormed away with tears tumbling down her cheeks, and her mother kindly picked up the magazine and finished reading. The stares she'd received after that performance would have made Faye Dunaway's Mommy Dearest character look like, "The Mother of the Century." She had warned her daughter about sneaking off with that (black) thug after school, and now she's showing her tough love. Maybe she might listen to her mother, or maybe next time all of them will listen to their mothers.

"Why did she even come?" whispered someone in the clinic.

"Her daughter must be a minor," her friend replied.

Diane had known that it was impolite to stare at people, but she was intrigued that there were so many different races of women under one roof. Statistics would make you believe that only black, young women were having abortions; which wasn't true. Not if they were to take (statistics) right now at this clinic.

The door creaked again. "Abby Kruchowski."

Diane recalled passing this place a thousand times, and she never imagined in a million years that she would have been sitting in here. She noticed one of the girls sitting by the television spitting into a Dixie Cup-how disgusting?

Lexis flopped down in the seat next to her, scooting underneath her. "It's cold in here."

"I guess you should be sis, you're wearing a short sleeve shirt and spandex pants," she giggled.

"Are you having doubts?"

"No."

Diane shook her head. "Look at that picture on the wall.

Alexis rolled her eyes, laughing, "What about it?" She hunched her shoulders. "What?"

"A picture of a woman holding a baby in an abortion clinic," she whispered. "And why do they have family magazines in here?"

Alexis closed her eyes, exhaled and replied to Conspiracy Cole, "You said yourself that they do more than abortions in here, they can promote life too?"

"I only said that to prove a point to her. Eighty percent of services that this clinic deals with are abortions, and you know it. The business is listed under Abortion Clinics so-"

"Alexis Brown," said the nurse.

"There is a God," she said loud. Her body started to tremble as she walked to the back room with her white, cotton gown in hand. "You were starting to get on my nerves," she walked away saying.

"So," Diane chuckled, as she picked up the magazine from the table to help calm her nerves. She was nervous about her sister getting the procedure done, but she couldn't let her know that. She had seen the nervousness in her eyes.

"Diane, is that you?"

The squeaky voice sounded familiar. She looked up. Kelly stood smiling off to the side of her. "Hey Kelly," she replied shocked, but not as shocked, as she was to see Juan strolling through the door behind her. What the fuck, she wondered.

He was appalled when he walked in and had seen Diane occupying a seat. She sat there stunned with her mouth wide-open and speechless... (Diane speechless?)

Alexis said she had scheduled an appointment for Thursday, not today, he thought. "We should leave," he whispered in Kelly's ear. She ignored his suggestion. It is time for Alexis to find out about us.

"I almost didn't recognize you without the glasses and the mushroom hair style," Kelly said.

"Yes, I cut my hair- as you can see," she said, touching her hair.

Juan decided to sit in a secluded area away from everyone behind a wall that had room for one chair.

He better had! She must be crazy standing here talking to me, and she just strolled in with my sister's boyfriend. I don't know what's going on, but the devil is always busy. He's working overtime on this one. I hope they're gone or her name is called before Lexis gets out. Oh shit! Here she comes."

She walked from the back with blood shot eyes; her eyelids were puffy like she had gotten into a fight with Mike Tyson. "I'm ready."

She walked past Juan not noticing him, and he waited for her to walk past and darted for the door.

"Where are you going Juan?" blurted Kelly.

"Juan?" wondered Alexis. She noticed the voice behind the caller. "Kelly?"

Kelly hightailed in behind him. "Juan, you better come back here and tell her," she explained. Everyone stared.

Alexis stood mannequin-like, looking traumatized until the information settled into her brain. It was now clear. Diane grabbed at her shirt, but missed it- outside she went and Diane accompanied her. Kelly and Juan stood in the parking lot arguing about why he wasn't going to tell Alexis about their baby.

"I'm not explaining anything to anyone! You do it!" Kelly said.

The pro-lifers were gone for the day, or on lunch break- either way the coast was clear.

Diane tried to convince Alexis why she shouldn't cause a scene with them; being black and in Eastpointe was one of them- *The Main One.* "Wait a minute," she yelled, walking in front of Alexis before she pushed her aside.

"What're you going to do," asked a smirking Kelly. Alexis wiped the smirk off of her face with a smack, and she fell to her knees. Kelly frantically jumped up yelling, but Diane told her to stand back, and let them handle it alone. She continued bumping and jumping around, expressing anger, (But not stupidity.) She kept her distance from Alexis' raging hands.

Juan told Kelly to get into the car, but not before Alexis began banging on the hood of his car and had put two dents into the driver's side door. She felt nauseated looking at them as a couple- her own first cousin and so-called boyfriend. She was hot under the collar, irate and demented all at the same time, which wasn't good at all. She didn't say a word- she couldn't speak- anger had her tongue- it took over, and it didn't want to talk, it wanted to see blood. Their blood.

A half piece of brick on the ground stuck out like its purpose for being there was strictly for her hand and his car. People stood around looking as the mad woman tried to destroy the moving vehicle. He shifted the transmission into reverse, but not fast enough because she had tagged his front windshield with the brick.

"You bitch!" He roared, burning rubber. As they pulled off, Kelly was on the inside of the car beating and cursing him out.

"Your trifling mama," Diane replied as the car sped off.

"Come on Alexis. Stand here, I have to go down there to that payphone and call a cab."

Still not speaking, Alexis leaned up against the side of the building. Her eyes filled with tears as she began weeping. Diane put her arm around her. "Cheer up, little sis. You got the chance to slap the fake Barbie into the middle of next week (like you always wanted to do.) You beautifully redecorated his pride and joy (like you said so many times that you wanted to do,) and you don't have to see his ugly face again, which is something I wanted," they giggled.

She smiled. "You might not be seeing his face, but you might see someone's face that looks like his. I didn't do it- I couldn't kill my baby."

"You mean you didn't?" she asked joyfully. She lifted her sister off her feet. "I'm sorry. Mama is going to be ecstatic!"

"Yeah, yeah," she mumbled. "She doesn't have to be sick every morning."

"Girl, you will be okay, and you are not supposed to be carrying on like that, and you're pregnant," she explained laughing. "You could've made my niece fall out from all that kicking and fighting."

"Will you go and call a cab? I'm hungry."

"You should be tired too."

"Funny."

"I thought you were going to pick up his car next," she said jokingly. "Super Woman," she laughed, walking towards the payphone.

Dear Diary,

It's never a dull moment in my family's life. Lexis is pregnant, and had planned on getting rid of the baby. When she went to the clinic, she couldn't do it after she got a glimpse of the baby on the ultrasound machine. To add spice to an already messed up situation, my cousin Kelly is pregnant by Juan as well, and they just happened to go to the clinic on the same day (talk about perfect timing.) Alexis had an appointment scheduled for Thursday, but they had a cancellation and scheduled it for Tuesday. He didn't want Alexis to keep the baby because he already had two kids. Kelly's baby is the third and Alexis (well, you can count.) Shaking my head- these females must be out of their minds. What are they fighting over? If he was so concerned about not having children then there's this thing called a condom, or a vasectomy; which would've put all his concerns aside and would save these women trips to the clinic and him money. He seems like the type of boy who lives carefree: a do-it-today, worry-about-it-tomorrow type of fellow. He obviously likes Kelly more because he went to the clinic with her, and she's fourteen weeks pregnant, so she's apparently keeping it (they went for confirmation.) Why are men so backwards? I've heard it through the grapevine that the baby she's carrying isn't even his. She's using him for his money and to get back at Alexis because they get along like water in an engine (see how long that works out for you.) Alexis is carrying his baby, and she likes him but he'd rather play house with Kelly (a phony, plastic individual; who's made-up from the top of her head to the bottom of her feet: horse hair, colored contacts, nail tips, eye-lashes, padded bras,) if you stripped the things that were purchased, she's average. Alexis isn't an ugly person, she could be pretty nerve-racking, but beautiful when she wants to be. (Did I just compliment her?) Kelly is crazy about name brands and would die before she stepped into school without make-up on and bragging rights of being the most fashionable student. The big dummy is twenty years old in the twelfth grade; she should be worried about finishing school before her baby catches up with her, rather than looking good and wearing designer jeans. Well, guess who's still in the twelfth grade? Kelly- yeah but she's an exception because she's so pretty... pretty dumb. All the hair, eyeliner and designer clothes in the world can't replace knowing that two negatives make a positive or that two wrongs don't make it right, so if you turn around and go left that might be right. (Huh?)☺ I just wanted to see if you were paying attention to me. My grandmother, The Cliché Queen, taught us that we are beautiful, strong women, who don't need for men to validate who we are because if we love ourselves unconditionally, we won't accept any bullshit from anyone else. My grandmother was raised by her (father's mother) grandmother (thank God) because the women in this family suffer from that "I'll take your man," syndrome. Aunt Max did it and now Kelly so I'd better be very careful when I get a boyfriend. I'm mad because I wished that I was there to see Lexis slap the dog shit out of Kelly. I wonder if she lost an eyelash or a contact lens. It must be something in the water and the women in my family are drinking it. Jeanette, Alexis, Kelly and (my cousin) Tiffany are all with child. I don't know who Jeanette's going to rely on to keep her baby while she works, but I can tell her who's not babysitting. I must return to the dungeon tomorrow night because school starts on Tuesday. Grandma took me to pick up my schedule. Of course I received a one to eight. Open to close- are you kidding me? First year in high school (I'm a DENBY TAR baby), and I have to be there all day long. I guess I'd better get my things because my vacation is officially over. Write in you soon Tamara

Four Months Later
December 23, 1990
EARLY ARRIVAL

Jeanette moved into the larger bedroom downstairs on the first floor because she was instructed to stay in bed until she had given birth to the baby. She had threatened a miscarriage twice within two months due to a weakened cervix. She needed to stay off of her feet until her due date, which was February 19, 1991. Everyone, well almost everyone, was excited about the arrival of the baby except Tamara. She had been bedridden but Tamara thought that she took the doctors' orders to the extreme. Jeanette bought a gold bell that she used to let Tamara know when she needed something. She wanted to take that bell, smash it and shove it up her nose every time she heard it ring.

She pictured her mother shaking that damn bell. Bring me a sandwich Tamara!" She would fix the sandwich. "Can you turn on a movie?" Ring! Ring! "I need you to come and change my bedpan." Ring! Ring! If I could kill her and get away with it, I would, she thought. Four more years and I'm out of here.

She had driven Tamara insane with the usage of her new gold bell. She came to the conclusion that she was either going to break her fingers or her hand. She chose the hand because if she broke her fingers, she would be able to slide the bell through her (broke) fingers to ring it. If she broke her hand, she won't be capable of moving it at all.

Yesterday, Jeanette called Tamara's principal and requested that she receive a two to seven hour schedule until she had the baby so she could help her out more at home. She didn't want to help out at all, and now she had to come home two hours early to deal with this shit. She stormed into the house, tossed her books onto the floor, and headed straight towards Jeanette's room. "I didn't get you pregnant so why must I be your full-time servant? This isn't fair!"

"Life isn't fair Tamara," explained Jeanette. "You don't want to help take care of me until I have the baby?"

She gave Jeanette a sassy look. "Hell No!"

She laughed. "If you take care of me now, I will leave this house and all my money to you, but you will have to take care of the baby."

She chuckled. "Oh gee, thanks a lot! All of this will be mine? This condemned house and your broken down Corsica, all three of your fake fur coats and your millions," she laughed. "The city will eventually come and tear this house down. Besides, you have what? Two hundred dollars in a savings account that me and your ugly baby will have to split. Not to mention, that I will have to raise a baby that I didn't create. No, thank you. I'll pass."

"Life is what you make it," said Jeanette.

"What did you make of your life?" She paused. "Not much, so save the knowledgeable speech for your stupid baby."

"Don't call my baby stupid. She's going to be smart," she said laughing.

Tamara mumbled. "If she's smart, as soon as she starts walking, she'll run away from this house."

"I heard that!"

"So what," she said, slamming the door. "I didn't stutter."

"You are a trip."

I wish that I could take a trip.

Even though she'd been released from school early today, (which she should have been happy about it, but wasn't) because next semester she would have to make up for the two classes that she was excused from.

She transferred the sloppily prepared sandwich, chips and beverage from the counter to the tray, and then to her room, almost knocking it over on her. "You and this ugly baby of yours is altering my damn life already, and it's not even born yet! I hate you!"

"What did we do know?"

"I have to take these two classes over, possibly even summer school because of you!" She flopped down in the chair. "I'm tired," she said, rubbing her sore feet.

Jeanette said with a smile, "I know you are. You can hate me but can you do it after you make me another sandwich, change this bedpan and bring my wash-up pan?" She looked at Jeanette screaming to the top of her lungs. "I HATE THIS HOUSE!!" She said slamming the door with all her strength.

That's one crazy child! She must get her attitude from her other people.

The phone rang ten times before she had answered it. Her counselor explained that she needed to provide the school with proof of her mother's condition from her physician. She felt relieved to have received the call because she had a legitimate reason to get out of the house before she killed Jeanette. She finished helping her mother, and then she headed straight to the clinic to pick up the health form. The rest of the day went smoothly.

The next morning, she stood in the school's main office waiting to give the secretary the signed form. The school's receptionist took the document from her hand and dialed the phone number on the paper to verify its authenticity. She stamped "Approval" on the form and an "Excused" stamp onto the pass.

Tamara slowly strolled to math class and that was when she decided that she wasn't going to allow Jeanette to make her suffer because she was miserable. She knew she had no choice but to help Jeanette out, but she was going to squeeze some fun time out for herself somehow.

Every day after school, she'd done her daily chores for Jeanette, homework, and helped herself to a serving of Charles (making out with him every other night.) Tonight, like most nights, she'd snuck him into her room as Jeanette slept. She wasn't worried about Jeanette walking upstairs because of her condition, but that didn't stop him from worrying.

"Happy sweet eighteenth birthday," she kissed him on the cheek.

"Thank you baby," he said, keeping his attention on the door. "What the fuck am I doing here? I must be crazy letting you convince me to come up here again. "

She kissed him, unfastening his pants. "Take these off and I will show you why you're here."

He enjoyed being with her, but not under these stressful circumstances.

"Stop being such a pussy," she retorted.

"Whatever girl, if Jeanette caught me up here she would kill me."

He had offered to pay for a hotel room but Tamara figured that she could've done better things with the money like buying cigarettes and that book by that new author Tameka Oliver.

"I can't leave this house anyway," she told him.

He wondered. (Yet was grateful) that Jeanette didn't wake up from all the noise they had made. To make matters worse, he was no longer a minor; he was a grown man now, and he thought of his father's words, whenever they were together. **"When you go to jail because you're messing around with that fast ass girl, don't call me or your mother to bail you out!"** At least his parents were aware of their friendship; Jeanette didn't have a clue. She had heard rumors that she liked Charles *many moons* ago, but she had no idea of what went on right underneath her nose in her home.

He had stretched across her bed half-naked wearing a watch and a pair of tube socks. He rolled over noticing that she was fully clothed, walking around.

"I need a cigarette."

"Dang," he said.

She snatched a cigarette out of its pack from the top drawer that was stashed underneath some clothes. She opened the window and parked herself on the ledge.

"What are you looking at?" she asked him, blowing the smoke outside.

He put on his black and red heart boxer shorts. "Why do you always rush and put your clothes back on after we have sex?" Most guys do stuff like that, not the girl. I wouldn't mind cuddling sometimes, he thought to himself.

She sat next to him after she had finished smoking her cigarette. "What do you want me to do? Lie around here naked so when Jeanette rings that fucking bell for me to do something, I have to rush and put my clothes on. That's too much shit to do. What should it matter to you? You got what you wanted."

He frowned. "You get on my nerves when you start acting like a bitch."

"Your mama," she cackled.

She continued to clean the filthy room. Her bedroom was always last to receive attention because she had to take care of everything else. She would be completely drained by the time she'd reached her room. All she wanted to do was hit the sheets.

She noticed him following her around the room with his eyes everywhere she had gone. She gathered his garments off of the floor, gently tossing them in his face. "You might want to put these on since I'm acting like a bitch."

He looked up at her, but didn't respond. He thought, Damn, I feel so used. He chuckled a bit. "Are you kicking me out?"

She gave him a half smile. "No, I'm not kicking you out yet."

"Yet," he asked surprisingly. He watched her as she switched around the room with her extra tight biker pants on. He became aroused as she bent over and he got another look at her breasts. "Come here."

"Stop," she continued to sweep the floor. "Move your feet before I sweep them, and you'll have back luck for ten years."

"I'm not superstitious," he chuckled inside. He grabbed his erect penis and freed it from an uncomfortable position. He said giddily, "Whoa, I was about to break my stuff off." He re-adjusted himself. "That's more like it."

"You always have your hands in your pants."

"My stuff is always coming out of my boxers."

"If you buy bigger boxer shorts then you'll solve that problem, or if you put your pants on your "stuff" won't flop out."

He retrieved his shirt (with the words "THE BEEF'S RIGHT HERE) from the bed and had put it on. "I guess I have to go home huh?"

"You don't have to go home, but you have to get the hell out of here," she said with a smile.

He grabbed her hips. "Are you kicking me out?"

She pushed him lightly away from her. "Move I can't clean up with you in the way."

He took the broom from her hands. "Give me this." He turned her around staring into her eyes. Look at his chocolate fine ass. The waves in his hair are so deep you could swim on top of one of them. His body has muscles in all the right places. In the dark his skin looks good, like a Hershey candy bar with the NUTS.

"Tamara?"

"What?" She playfully snatched the broom back from him.

"Tamara, I love you," he confessed.

Those words stopped her dead in her tracks, not because she was excited that he had finally said them to her, especially since night-after-night she'd dreamed of hearing him say that to her. That was a childhood fantasy of hers that she had given up on about three years ago. The only reason why she had spent time with him was to keep her company and to curb her "other" appetite from time-to-time. Her back was turned to him when he had professed his love, but she kept on cleaning hoping that he wouldn't say it again. She pictured the way his mouth moved as he said those three (deep conditioned) words. "Look at all this stuff in my room," she nervously grabbed the last cigarette from the pack.

She's a trip because she knew she heard me tell her that I loved her. I'm going to tell her again. "I love you, Tamara."

She swallowed, making the smoke travel down the wrong windpipe. She coughed uncontrollably. She coughed so hard; it looked like she was going to spit out a hairball. She quickly tossed the cigarette out the window grasping for air. He ran over to her and had struck her in the back a few times.

"Are you okay?"

She tried to reply but nodded instead as tears rolled down her face. She retrieved her beverage from on top of her nightstand. She cleared her throat. "Look at what you made me do? Stupid."

"You were about to die because I said I love you," he laughed. "I take it back then."

"Good," she looked angrily at him. "That's not funny ni**a," clearing her throat twice. She stuck her head out of the window inhaling some fresh air. She looked up at the stars and mumbled to herself.

"What you say?" he asked.

"We haven't been seeing each other long enough for you to love me."

"What?" he chuckled. "I've known you for a long time. What are you talking about?"

"I don't know. See how you got me talking? I can't even think straight."

"You never thought straight. I've known you longer than you probably have known yourself."

"I've known you long enough to know that you're full of shit. Okay, funny man- finish getting dressed and leave," she commanded.

He walked on her heels. "Why am I full of shit? What did I do? Answer the question."

She pushed him and made him fall backwards onto the bed. "You don't love me."

"How come you can't answer my question? Here, I'll ask you again. Do you love me?"

She sat on the bed. "I-I- love your sex," she said with a big smile on her face.

"Well, I'm glad about that but do you love," he pointed to himself, "me?"

She placed her hands over her eyes like she was shy. He moved her hands from her face. "You don't do you?" He laughed softly to himself to cover up the hurt. "I can't believe this?" He quietly sat there in disbelief as he learned her true feelings about him. His trigger finger rested on his nose while his other fingers propped his face up. "I really can't believe this," he repeated.

She moved closer to him. "What do you want me to say?" She laughed. "Are you mad at me?"

"Say you love me."

"No Charles, love is overrated baby. That's a four-letter word made up to control people lives. You won't do this if you love me... I thought you loved me, but you went and did that! If people didn't put so much stock in that word, people wouldn't get hurt. Love is a feeling, but so is temptation. I think people give in to temptation more than they give in to love, why bother?"

"Have you ever been in love before?"

"Yeah," she mumbled.

"With whom," he asked.

She smiled. "None of your bees wax."

He had put her in a headlock. "With whom," he repeated.

"You," she replied kind of loud. "We have to tone it down."

"Why do you try to hide your true feelings all the time? If you loved me, what happened?"

"I thought I loved you, when I was ten years old. I tried to tell you I liked you, but you didn't pay me any attention because you went with Adr..."

He cut her off saying, "Adrian."

"You were so in love with her, you probably shit out hearts for months. When I spoke to you, you just threw up your funky hands and kept walking, like I didn't matter to you."

"What did you want me to do? I was fourteen years old, and you were what- Two? I would've..."

"I know. You would've been underneath the jail cell."

"No, your grandfather would've killed me first."

"My grandfather wasn't the one that you should've have been concerned about. He was a big man, but he wouldn't kill a fly."

"Didn't he go to the army?"

"He did, but of course he would kill to save his own life, but he just wouldn't kill to be doing it."

"I don't care what you say, if I would've talked to you, your grandfather would've killed me and my friends would've been teasing me. I'm not a predator."

She chuckled. "I'm telling you, he wouldn't have liked it, but he wouldn't have killed you. I didn't say for us to go together anyway, I knew I was too young, but you didn't have to ignore me like you did."

"I didn't ignore you. I thought you were cute, but you were just too young."

"I'm still too young."

He said with a devilish grin on his face. "You don't act young? What's your problem with me?"

"What?"

"Why do you act so funny?"

She smiled. "I don't know what you mean?"

"Bitchy?"

"My life consists of cleaning up after grown people that don't appreciate it. I have to cook for Jeanette. Well, I've always cooked for her, now I have to wait on Jeanette hand and foot. I never get a break."

"What's wrong with that? She's pregnant now. She won't be like that forever."

"Hush, you're too loud," she said. "You come take care of her then."

"I will."

"Anyway, if I did love you- I would never tell you because once you confirm it people go crazy. They act like just because you love them, they own you. No one owns me, but me. I'd rather have fun, and go our separate ways once it's over. I don't want any strings attached because that makes things really complicated. Say tomorrow, you met a girl that you liked, y'all dug each other- if we go together, "being a dog like most boys are," you're eventually going to cheat and rather being committed to me, you would be free to pounce on her, me and anybody else you liked as long as you didn't bring anything back to me. However, if we're committed to each other, and you cheated on me," she frowned at him, "and I found out, all hell would break loose. Trust me."

He asked, "What do you want from me?"

"For you to do whatever I need done, no matter what it is. Whenever I tell you to do it, by any means necessary, or I will keep my stuff in my pants."

He giggled lightly. "You always blackmail me with that one." He laughed. "What kind of girl are you? Who doesn't want a commitment?"

"What kind of guy are you? You're eighteen and you want a commitment? You're a baby. I might see a boy tomorrow that I might want to get with and chances are, if I want to I will, so it's best that we keep this the way it is. Don't expect nothing more than what I have been giving you, (she pointed between his legs), and I won't expect anything more than your eight inch ..."

"Tamara, did you hear that?"

"Sssh, I thought I just heard something too, be quiet," she whispered. "Something just fell downstairs."

She laughed at Charles because he reminded her of Shaggy from Scooby Doo.

"Your mama is coming," he said as he hurried up and put on his shoes. He grabbed the sheets and started tying them together. "I'll go out of the window," he said nervously.

She snatched the sheets from him. "Don't have a cow dude! You're such a chicken."

"I'd rather be a scared chicken who lives than a dead one. I'll be sitting on top of the dinner table tonight, and she's pregnant too. She'll eat me with one gobble."

She shook her head. "Will you chill the fuck out? Calm down man.

I'm about to go down there and see what she wants. She probably wants something to eat, or I have to change her bedpan. Relax Scooby."

"She's coming upstairs," Charles said.

"Tamara," Jeanette yelled.

"I'll be right back. Don't move."

Please Be Kind And Rewind

REWIND> The pain in Jeanette's back refused to ease up. I feel as though I'm trapped in a pair of vise grips, she thought. Going back to sleep or even resting comfortably was out of the question. She tried breathing techniques; nothing seemed to work. She decided that it was time to inform Tamara of her pain.

It was pitch black in her room. She could not see her hands in front of her face. The only thing visible was the alarm clock that read 10:30.

"Tamara forgot to turn on the nightlight. Damn her ass."

The pain intensified from her lower back to the center of her neck. She tossed and turned hoping that she could have found a position that relieved the pressure. No position worked out for her. The pain formed quick, sharp, needle like cramps in her abdomen. She balled up into the fetal position with that being the only way to get a "little" comfort.

"If I could only get some sleep, I'll go to the hospital first thing in the morning. I can't expect to have a pain free pregnancy like I did with Tamara." She exhaled. All babies are different, she convinced herself. "Everything will be all right," she mumbled. Her eyes had adjusted to the dark, so she could now she the gold bell on the night stand.

"If I can reach it," she knocked it down. "Ouch, what's wrong with me?"

She felt an enormous amount of pressure in her vagina. She placed her hands between her legs calling out for Tamara after she'd felt a watery substance gush out. She didn't hear Tamara making her way down the stairs, so she tried to get the bell again. "Shit!"

She sniffed her fingers for an odor. There was no smell.

She sat in the middle of the bed contemplating on getting up. She really did not have a choice. Her legs have not been on the side of the bed in months, it actually felt weird.

"What is Tamara doing up there?" She wondered. "These must be contractions and I'm about to lose my baby," she said nervously.

She pictured Damarcus being in prison and not at home with her like he had always promised her. "I'm counting to five and I have to get up. I can't take this." She counted to seven and stood up. Her legs felt like noodles. She used the wall as support as she carefully staggered to the living room. She knocked down the heart shaped picture frame that was a photograph of her and Damarcus at Metro Park. Those were the good old days. That's when she noticed the puddle of blood that she stood in. She became woozy and the room started to fade to black.

Tamara finally decided to go downstairs, and she discovered Jeanette lying on the floor, in the exact location where Damarcus bled to death. She tapped her face and called her name until she came to.

"Call 9-1-1," she whispered.

"What's the number again?" she asked.

She exhaled. "Stop playing."

"Don't get an attitude with me lady," she chuckled. She went into the kitchen humming a Prince Song (not picking up the receiver until she finished her favorite part,) "She's always in my hair. My hair! Now, I will call." She killed two valuable minutes humming instead of calling because she had yelled at her. "You don't yell at a person if you need them to do something for you."

Operator: "9-1-1, what's your emergency?"

Tamara: "There's a lady here having a baby."

Operator: "I have your location as 12761 Flanders. Is that correct?"

Tamara: "Yeah," she answered sarcastically.

Operator: "I'm dispatching an ambulance right now. What's the age of the pregnant person?"

Tamara: "How old are you Jeanette?"

Jeanette answered. "Thirty-four," she groaned.

Operator: How many months is she? And do you see the baby's head crowning, yet?"

Tamara: What? Crowning? I wasn't looking down there for any crowning! Are you crazy? How many months are you?

Jeanette said, "Almost seven. Will they please send an ambulance? I'm having contractions and I'm bleeding! Can you not ask me anymore questions?"

Tamara: "Did you hear that? She needs your help but she's talking about don't ask her anymore questions."

Operator: "Please ask her if her water has broken? Is she lying down? If not I need you to do a few things for me- what's your name?"

Tamara: "Yes," she replied. "And yes, what do I have to do and what difference does my name make?"

Operator: "Okay, can you get a towel wet it and place it on her head. Elevate her legs on some pillows until help arrives."

Tamara: "Yeah okay, I hear them now," she explained lying.

Operator: "Okay good. Don't han-," she tried to finish her sentence.

Tamara quickly said, "Thanks," and hung up.

Oh shit, I forgot about Charles! She quickly ran into the bathroom-soaked the towel and tossed (the dripping towel) to her. "Put that on your big forehead Jeanette." She snatched two pillows off of the sofa saying, "Put that under your head and feet." She had gotten her sandwiches off the table and opened the door because she really heard the ambulance's sirens.

"Here they come now, thank God, all that moaning and groaning is working my nerves."

"Where's the person in-"

She rudely interrupted him. "She's over there," she pointed on the floor, and proceeded upstairs. "Any questions, you might have to ask her."

They looked at each other shaking their heads.

When she reached her room, Charles had vanished. He had tied two sheets together and disappeared like David Copperfield. "He's so scary," she chuckled.

They worked rapidly on Jeanette because she had lost a great deal of blood and definitely needed to see a doctor.

"Hello," the lady technician yelled upstairs for Tamara.

"Yeah," she angrily answered.

"We are transporting her to Hut-."

"Hutzel Hospital, I know!"

The two technicians exchanged baffled looks again at each other (because of the rude girl's attitude.) They placed the weird girl's mother onto the stretcher. "Okay, let's move her out on my count."

Tamara turned the volume up on her headphones as she stuffed her face eating her sandwich. *Guilt* crept through her brain because of the way that she had treated her mother, but she quickly dismissed it by saying, "That wasn't my fault- I didn't make Jeanette pregnant or weak. I have to go downstairs and lock the door," she sighed. "Man."

DIARY ENTRY 5

May 9, 1991

Dear Diary,

Hello Diary. It's been a long time. A new year has begun and is damn near over. I haven't written in you because with school, babysitting, cleaning up, Charles and television- there isn't any time available. I'm miserable, and if I could find another word that's worse than 'miserable' then that's what I would be. The situation is crazy now since I have to watch Lasha. Next school year I have to take those two extra classes, and I don't know how that's going to work out because I keep the "WHINER," with her hollering little ass. She drives me up a wall, and I don't complain about it because it won't do any good. I constantly fall asleep in class all the time. My grades are drastically going down; I went from A's to C's instantaneously.

Jeanette was late on her day job six times and was laid off. She worked seven days for sixteen years, zero absence for this company, and before she started having car trouble and Lasha's appointments; they loved her- so she thought. She didn't mind because she could get her unemployment benefits and was able to be at home with the "Little Whiner," but I have to see after her because once she goes to sleep, she's out like a turn signal light bulb. Charles is becoming a little nerve wrecking; he's mad because I still don't want to be boyfriend and girlfriend. I really don't have time to be a girlfriend because I'm too busy playing mother (to my sister.) That's why whenever I'm able to get away to grandma's house I run like a quarterback. Alexis and I still agree to disagree on everything when I go and visit. Ashley, her daughter, came out weighing twelve pounds and eleven ounces, ripping her mother a new ass hole. Ashley is a good baby in comparison to "Little Whiner," feed her, and she's sleep for a while. Grandma keeps Ashley while Alexis goes to work and school, but I'm stuck with big mouth. Juan hasn't seen as much as a picture of his baby. Kelly had her baby and Juan found out that the baby wasn't his- it was his cousin's-you see how karma works? Paul, his brother comes over to see and bring Ashley gifts, but I think he's coming to visit Alexis also. I heard that he had liked Alexis, but Juan got next to her first. (Snooze, you lose.) Lynette continues to strip and I get hush money from her every month because grandma still is in the dark about that.

Jeanette had the house fixed up before Lasha was released from the hospital. She had to stay in the hospital for eight weeks because her lungs weren't strong enough to breathe without oxygen. It took for Princess Lasha to be born before she worked on the house. I have to do homework and study for a test (that I will probably fail.) Until next time.

DOOMS DAY
September 10, 1991
Tuesday- 7:45 a.m.

Today was another gloomy, boring, rainy day. The streets were filled with puddles of water from the rain. You couldn't tell that it was morning because it was still dark outside. Jeanette's window was cracked wide enough for a small breeze to come through and ruffle the blinds. Tamara relaxed in the bed listening to the raindrops hit the awning and the windowsill outside. She counted the seconds after the flash of lightning struck to see how long it took for the thunder to come. The windows shook so she decided to put on her headphones to listen to some music. She loved when it rained, but hated the thundering and lightning that followed. What she loved most was the scent of fresh rain once it aired out her small (stuffy) room.

Jeanette was downstairs dead to the world. She was a terrible person to have to occupy a bed with. When she was younger she had the entire bed to herself because no one wanted to sleep beside her. She snored, kicked, punched and pissed excessively over herself and the unlucky guest who had to sleep with her. That's why Lasha slept in a crib, in the bedroom upstairs next to Tamara's room because she slept light.

One day last week, Tamara heard a loud *boom,* and then a loud cry, because Lasha had rolled out of the bed, or Jeanette kicked her out. Either way her sleeping arrangements had to change from that day forward. She had a big knot on her head for a few days and was more irritable all that day.

The rain fell harder making it impossible to see the house across the street, and the thunder made the windows tremor. If you hadn't known any better you would've sworn that it had struck the house. The loud sound of thunder startled Jeanette and she snapped out of her coma. Have I been up yet to feed Lasha? What time is it? She wondered as she rubbed her burning eyes. She rolled over and glanced at the alarm clock. It was one of those days that you wanted to stay in bed all day and not be disturbed by anyone, maybe grab a bite to eat and head straight back to bed.

Tamara was stretched out across the bed listening to Al Green's "Love and Happiness" she hugged her Winnie the Pooh teddy bear. She'd bought Lasha a matching teddy bear from the dollar store on Gratiot three days ago. Al Green's voice started to drag because the batteries were dying. Good thing she had followed her mind and bought two packs of batteries the other day. A huge percentage of her allowance (if not all of it) went on batteries, candy and cassette tapes.

"Oh shit! I've overslept and my baby is probably starving." Jeanette ran into the kitchen and took out an eight-ounce bottle from the refrigerator. She loved having a reason to open her new refrigerator. She was so proud of her gift from her baby sister. She wondered where Lynette got the money for this expensive gift, but she'd accepted it gratefully. She went into the kitchen drawer to take out *the purple* lighter for the stove. She smiled to herself; she forgot she had a new stove too. "Oh shoot- I forgot that I don't have to use the lighter anymore." She tested the bottle on the back of her hand. "Ouch, that's too hot!" She put some cold water into a cup and dropped the bottle into it. She walked up the stairs humming, Shirley Murdock's song "As We Lay." The song played on the radio last night, and she hadn't been able to get it out of her head. That was her mother's favorite song.

She opened the door peeping into the room. "Good she's still sleeping," she whispered. Lasha was lying in the crib with her face towards the teddy bears. "She was really tired. Good morning, Mama's Pooh Bear. Time to get up and eat little mama," she said, walking over to the diaper changing table to get a diaper. She must've been real tired because she has never slept past six thirty before, thought Jeanette.

She reached into the crib picking her up, but there was no sign of life in her little body. She immediately started CPR.

"This can't be happening!" Her body had lain limp, cold and non-responsive. Her face was a dark blue color. She softly shook her hoping that would wake her up. Nothing worked.

"Tamara!!! OH MY GOD! LASHA. Tamara!"

She started giving the baby CPR again. Maybe I wasn't doing it right. She rehearsed the CPR steps that she'd learned when she took the class at American Red Cross.

Tamara removed the headphones because she thought she heard Jeanette's voice. "What does she want now?" she mumbled.

She stood in the hallway watching Jeanette lose her mind. "What are you doing?" she yelled.

"My baby, she's not breathing!" Jeanette hysterically had given her two quick breaths followed by thirty chest compressions using her two fingers like she was trained to do. "Come on baby girl," she mumbled.

"What happened to her," Tamara screamed.

"Call for help! Oh Lord! It's not working!"

Tamara called for help and then she called her grandmother. "Grandma something's wrong with Lasha. She's not breathing," Tamara said nervously.

"WHAT?"

"I just called the ambulance, and they're on their way. Grandma! She's not breathing! Come over here!"

"Here I come," Barbara replied troubled.

Jeanette sobbed, rocking back and forth as she held Lasha in her arms on the floor. "What happened to my baby? What did you do to my baby?"

"What did I do? You were the last one in here with her so what did YOU do to her?"

Jeanette yelled. "I HATE YOU! I didn't do anything! You did something to my baby!"

"When I laid her down she was fine last night," Tamara explained.

Tamara heard the sirens from the ambulance truck in front of the house. She went downstairs and opened the door. Jeanette sat there rocking her with this mortified (crazed) look upon her face. "Lasha, wake up for mama!"

"I can't believe the same male technician from last time is back," she mumbled. "Are you the only EMT working on the eastside?"

"No, we were the closest to the scene," said Head. Murkowski and Head stormed into the house carrying their equipment. "Where's the baby?" asked Murkowski.

"Go upstairs the first room on your left." Tamara stood there with her eyes full of tears. "Oh- what have-"

"What's the matter with the baby ma'am? Can I see her," asked Head. She snatched away from Head. "No, she's gone. Don't touch my baby!" she yelled. Murkowski held out her hands. "Give us the baby."

"You're just trying to take her away from me! Get your hands off of me!"

Tamara leaned up against the wall in the hallway by the room as a thousand different emotions ran through her mind and body.

"Oh no, I can't breathe," Jeanette fainted. She hit her head hard on the floor as the reality of her baby dying hit her.

Head ran over to her. "What's her name?"

"Jeanette."

He tapped her shoulder. "Jeanette, are you okay?" He placed an oxygen mask over her face. A few seconds passed and she woke up yelling and screaming. "Where's my baby?" She snatched the mask off her face as she jumped up and went over to her baby. "NO!"

She yelled for everyone to get out of the room. "You weren't here to save my baby so all of you get the hell out this room! Don't touch my baby!" She slammed the door.

"Let's step over her." Murkowski asked Tamara, "What happened?"

"Are you the police too?"

"No," answered Head.

Murkowski was already on her CB notifying the authorities. It was Standard Operating Procedure whenever someone was D.O.A when "they" arrived. She was not in the mood to deal with Tamara's sarcasm today.

"Do what you have to do first, and then ask me questions," she said sarcastically as she started cleaning her nails out.

"We have to fill out a report about what happened here that's all honey," Head explained.

"So what happened?" he asked again.

"All I know is this morning, Jeanette woke up-"

He interrupted. "Is Jeanette your mother?"

"Are you going to let me finish or not?"

"Sorry," he smiled.

She rolled her eyes at him. "When she woke up Lasha wasn't breathing. Her face was all blue and Jeanette started screaming. I called y'all and that's all I know."

"Okay, thank-you ma'am. We're going to stay outside until the examiner arrives."

"My name is Tamara. I'm not a ma'am."

Tamara cracked the door wide enough to see that she was changing the baby's diaper talking to her. "Oh Jesus, Jeanette's going nuts," she mumbled.

Barbara, Aunt Ann and Uncle Jay stormed into the house because the door was wide open. "Jeanette!"

"We're up here grandma!"

You heard Barbara screaming once she caught a glimpse of her grandchild lying in her mother's arms lifeless. They all held each other as Jeanette stood in the middle holding the baby.

"Mama, why did this happen? Mama! Oh Mama! Why did this happen to my baby?"

"Dear God help us," said Barbara.

I have to go outside somewhere and smoke, thought Tamara. "I'll be back."

Damaurcus' mother, Charisse burst into the house almost knocking Tamara down. "Where's Jeanette?" Tamara pointed upstairs.

She didn't know actually what was wrong because a neighbor called telling her that the ambulance was at Jeanette's house.

"No, not my baby," Charisse started scratching herself like she had fleas. She did this when she was really nervous about something. Tamara couldn't stomach the sounds that came from upstairs any longer. She stood on the side of the house in her pajamas underneath her umbrella in the rain. The medical examiner pulled in front of the house writing something down on a notepad. She put out the cigarette and walked onto the front porch.

"Hello," he said.

She waved. He walked towards the door wearing a black raincoat carrying his doctor bag looking like *Dr. Death* himself. Tamara felt a spooky aura about him.

"Go right in. Go to the first room to the left, but let someone know that you're here before you go up there, or you'll need a medical examiner for yourself."

"Thanks for the warning," he snickered.

He took heed and knocked on the door, and Barbara answered it.

"Who is it?" she yelled, peeping out the window.

He explained who he was, and she let him in to do his job. However, it wasn't going to be easy. Everyone vacated the room except for Jeanette. He examined Lasha, and asked her a series of questions. He came to the preliminary conclusion that suffocation was the cause of death. She must've turned over on her teddy bears and couldn't turn back over, and she suffocated.

Jeanette held her hands over her face as he explained what he determined had happened. "I've seen tragedies like this happen before, and I'm so sorry. There was another possibility as well; her baby could have died from SIDS.

That's when the infant brain's forgets how to breathe naturally, and they suffocate."

She relaxed on the twin-sized bed next to Lasha, rocking back and forth crying. This was too much for her to handle.

The doctor thought, I hate my job at times like this. I feel so bad for the family. He opened the door. "I'll be back." He touched Barbara's shoulder and asked her, "Can I speak to you alone?"

"Sure."

"I represent Swanson's Funeral Home." He passed her a business card. "You can call Mr. Nestle to get the arrangements together if you didn't have a place in mind. You have my deepest condolences. I just buried my own mother two weeks ago."

"I'm sorry to hear that," Barbara said.

He forced a smile. "She lived a good life."

He went out to the van and brought back the Gurney and a body bag. "I'm going to leave this down here so she won't see me put the baby in it. I have to take her and that's always the hardest part for the parents."

"It'll be okay. She has us."

"I'm sorry Shay. Mama's sorry. I couldn't help you."

Ann and Jay tried getting Jeanette off the floor with the baby, but she refused.

"I don't want to get up now."

Barbara wiped her tears. "Baby, get up. He's here to get the baby."

She held her tighter. "No one's taking my baby from me. I'm going with her. I want to go with her!"

Aunt Ann said, "What about Tamara?"

"She doesn't love me. She did this!"

Everyone in the house had to grab a limb; because she started kicking and screaming. She bit the medical examiner on his right hand and kicked Charisse in the stomach. Ann and Barbara grabbed Jeanette as he took the baby downstairs. Jeanette tried with all her strength to break loose but they sat on her. "I want to look out and see my baby!"

"You don't need to see her," said Charisse.

"Don't tell me what I need to see!"

"Let her go," explained Barb. "Let her look out of the window."

The medical examiner pulled off in a hurry, leaving the gurney behind. All he had time for was to get the baby and place her in the bag before Jeanette had gotten loose. They released her.

Jeanette was irritated; she had broken everything that she had touched. She ran into the bathroom and locked the door.

"Jeanette!" called Barbara. "Open the door."

She searched in the medicine cabinet for any pills to take. "Go away Mama."

"Please open up the door."

THE MISSI G PAGES

DIARY E TRY

Sunday

Dear Diary,

Grandma stayed a week over to the house after Lasha died. The family constantly came to visit Jeanette and grandma. I stayed in my room because I have never seen so many people under one small roof before in all my years. I didn't recognize half of those people. They just wanted to be nosey and hear what had happened to the baby. Everyone who came brought plenty of food with them. We had enough fish, chicken and spaghetti to last an entire year. Grandma stored most of the food in the freezer for a later date. I believed that Jeanette honestly appreciated the fact that people came to see about her, but she wasn't in the frame of mind for guests, but they kept coming anyway. Monday, Grandma and William went to the funeral home to make the arrangements. I overheard grandma saying that she decided on a closed casket because she didn't think that Jeanette would be able to handle it being open. On Tuesday, Nia and Nikki came over to see about me. I told them that I was all right, but they insisted that I was trying to put up a strong shield for them. Nia hadn't been over here in months, I told her that she should've have stayed where she was and that made her cry. Like always, I hurt her little sensitive ass feelings again. I told them that I didn't feel like being bothered; so whatever I say, so be it. Everyone has days that they'd rather not be bothered. I have more of those days than normal people I guess, but that's just me. This morning Jeanette was doing a little better, or so we thought, but she had us fooled. She ate some breakfast today for the first time since Lasha died. She even laughed and spoke a few words to Diane and Marion. When nighttime came, grandma went downstairs into the kitchen to get some water, and she found Jeanette stretched out on the floor. I heard grandma screaming and then Diane. "Call for help!" Next to Jeanette laid an empty prescription bottle of Motrin 600 pills. I just closed my eyes and turned up the music in my headset. I know she has every right to be upset because she had lost her child, but she's grieving worse than grandma did when granddaddy died. And she knew him longer than Jeanette knew Lasha. Okay, that sounds a little heartless. I wondered would she have acted this way if it was me who had died, instead of her precious little baby. After the ambulance people came, thank goodness it wasn't Head and Murkowski. They had to pump Jeanette's stomach because she had taken thirteen pills. It was a good thing that grandma had gone downstairs at that precise moment or Jeanette would've been "a goner", especially if we were here alone because I never go around the house like that. Jeanette's not going to stop until she kills her foolish self. They put her in a psychiatric hospital to keep a close watch over her for two days. She needed them now more than ever. She loved that baby a million times more than she could possibly love me. I'll never forget that day when she told me that she hated me. I knew she felt that way about me, but I never imagined that she would confess it around the family. If she doesn't like me- why in the world would she make me come here and stay with her? I was fine where I was. All of these years of cooking and cleaning like a slave, was her way of punishing me because deep down inside she was full of resentment towards me. That's why she never bought me anything, or took me anywhere, because she hated my guts. Well if that's the case, then I guess the feelings were mutual. Overall, I still had the last laugh; she doesn't know it yet, but I did. I took away things that she held in high regards. There's a real thin line between love and hate. Operation Get Revenge part 2 is complete. Now, I will start on part 3.

The Funeral

Saturday September 14, 1991.

The morning sun played hide-go-seek with the clouds, as it rained off and on. It shouldn't have been a surprise because it rained every day this week, adding sadness to an already depressed situation. It didn't rain half as much in April like it was supposed to, but it made up for it this month. It seemed like all the tears shed for Lasha must've poured down from the clouds. Why does it feel like whenever you are sad, it rained making you feel worse? Maybe that's just the way it seemed, but the closer the clock moved towards nine, the harder the rain came down.

Jeanette and Tamara stayed over to Barbara's house the night after Jeanette tried to commit suicide for a second time. She figured that she needed twenty-four hour care after being released from the hospital. Jeanette hadn't looked forward to going back to the house because it held too many memories. Memories that she wasn't prepared to confront right now. Her man was somewhere locked up and had not taken the time to drop a line to say, "hey, I'm still breathing baby" and now her only "gift from him" was gone as well. She didn't feel that she had anything to live for. She was alone and felt guilty for living.

Barbara monitored her every ten minutes checking on her until she fell asleep. Most nights, she crawled into bed with her because it was easier than running back and forth every thirty minutes. Barbara hadn't had much sleep since the baby died. Babysitting her fragile daughter all the while grieving herself was a challenge. She still mourned the loss of her husband even though some days were better than others but with each passing day she healed.

Today, she was stretched across her mother's bed gazing at the ceiling as visions of her boyfriend and child played across her tired, closed, teary eyes like a home video. Her mental visualization displayed a few good images, but switched to images of a lifeless infant. Without checking the time, she felt her heart as it started to pound harder and faster knowing what she soon had to endure. Viewing her precious little baby in that casket was going to take whatever ounce of strength that she had left. Her mind informed her that it was time to get ready because she heard the family scampering around downstairs. Her mind sent the signals to get up, but her nerves were being stubborn.

Tamara looked intently outside her window peering down at four birds bathing in a puddle of water as one *clever* bird skipped across the grass pecking the ground for worms. She heard Alexis holler that the funeral drivers were on their way.

Everyone who had planned on riding in the family cars for the service met up at Grandma's house. Marion and Diane arrived at nine twenty sharp to pick up Jeanette. They headed to the funeral home because Jeanette didn't want to ride in the funeral car. She imagined that would have made the reality of where she was headed soak in faster.

She stepped out wearing one of those big white *"church"* hats with the lace concealing her face. She had on a white and gold pinned striped, two-piece pants suit. She asked for the immediate family members to dress in white. She had expressed her desire that no one wear black because she felt that black represented sadness. "She was my angel, so I want us to wear white because of its purity and angelic nature." Everyone obliged with her wishes, well, almost everyone.

Jeanette rode in the front passenger's seat staring out of the window wondering where the people were going at nine thirty on a Saturday morning. Perhaps to work, she assumed. Diane flicked on the radio to kill the quietness in the car. Ironically, Shirley Murdock's "As We Lay" was on the radio. Jeanette burst out into tears.

"What? What happened?" asked Diane. "What's wrong?"

"Oh my God!" yelled Jeanette. The way she screamed, Diane didn't know what to think.

She nervously pulled over to the side. "What's the matter?"

"That was the song that I was singing before I found out that my baby was-" she cried, "My baby was gone...."

"Turn it off," he yelled. Marion started massaging her shoulders from the backseat. "Let it out sis."

She relaxed her head on the headrest. Jeanette tried the relaxing technique her nurse at (the mental hospital) taught her to do for twenty minutes. She rubbed her temples in a circular motion counting with her eyes closed until they arrived.

Diane touched her leg gently. "We're here."

She couldn't seem to stop the tears from falling down her face. Even with her eyes closed tightly they still formed.

"You two go in and I'll be in shortly."

"Are you sure sis?" asked Diane. She wiped her tears away and nodded. "I'm sure."

She thought, get it together. You can do this, all you need is a little more courage, and it'll all be over soon. She went inside her purse and pulled out two pills (wrapped in a napkin) and a half of pint of Christian Brothers. She took the pills and realized from looking in the side view mirror that the rest of the family had pulled into the parking lot. Other mourners had begun pulling into the lot as well. Barbara jumped out of the car before the driver parked to come and get Jeanette.

"Come on Nette."

The closer Jeanette got to the door the more she felt like she was going to faint. "Mama I can't do it," she held onto her mama tightly.

"Yes, you can baby. I felt the same way when your father passed. We can do this together."

The lines were long to get into the funeral home so Barbara yelled and pushed making a path, to get through.

"Excuse me! Can the mother of the child be the first person in line please? Excuse us! Excuse me!"

The people split like the Red Sea and allowed them to pass through. "Thank you very much."

"Aunt Barbara is so mean," said Walter.

"She sure is. I can't stand her," remarked his twin sister, Wendy.

Two sets of double glass doors held the key to whether or not Jeanette kept her sanity, or this would have been her last half normal thought before the next set of doors would be metal, kept locked, with white padded walls and a matching one-piece suit with restraints.

That distinguished funeral home smell of flowers and death immediately socked your nose once you opened the second set of doors. Soft music played from the speakers located in each corner on the wall. On the left as soon as you entered was a black billboard that had the names of the deceased and time of the family hour and funeral service.

She noticed: LASHA JEAN BROWN
FAMILY HOUR 11:00 a.m. - 12:00 p.m.
FUNERAL SERVICE 12:00 p.m. - 1:00 p.m.
ROOM 100 Straight ahead

Jeanette felt her knees buckle underneath her and almost lost her balance. Her heart pounded forty times a second. She closed her eyes and started counting.

"One, two, three..."

A set of twelve brown leather chairs sat in the hallway on the left side of the room: for those who wanted to be there for support but couldn't stomach seeing a dead child's body. In the opposite corner, there was a book for the guests to sign as they entered the room to sit down.

"Come on Nette," Barbara placed her left arm over her shoulder. "You ready to go in? Let's pray first."

She managed to crack a smile. "Yes mama. It will be over soon."

"Yes it will. And we can begin to heal."

They walked through another set of doors as their family sat in the first two rows. Behind the white and gold two and a half foot casket was a beautiful sixteen by thirteen photo of nine-month-old Lasha smiling at the camera for her mother. It was taken after she had gotten her ears pierced.

The funeral director passed out obituaries as the guests entered. She gave directions on where they could sit.

A lady dressed in white passed out Kleenex and fans to the people who needed them. Jeanette motioned for the director.

"Why is my baby's coffin closed?"

"Your mother thought that it would've been better for you all to deal with it if it was closed."

"I want it opened- and I want it opened now!"

"Are you sure?" asked the director.

"Yes, I'm sure."

"Are you sure you want to do that Nette?"

"Yes mama."

Jeanette and Barbara followed behind the director.

As the man came from the back and opened the small casket, a chorus of grief consumed room 101.

They should have kept it closed, Jay thought.

Jeanette decided to let her mother view the body first because she wasn't prepared to see her yet. She looked away.

"OH Boogie," cried Barbara. She stood over the casket looking down at her little Boogie Bear. She thought back to the very first time she had seen her squirming around in the incubator fighting for a chance to live, and now she's lying in a casket (grudgingly hand-picked by Barbara herself) engraved in gold: Grandma's Boogie Bear forever. She whispered in Lasha's ear and kissed her cold cheek.

"Tell your grandfather I said hello. I know he'll take good care of you until I get there. I love you. I can't take this." Barbara stood on the side of Jeanette praying for strength to help her daughter as she walked towards the baby. She rested on her mother's shoulder, as she had gotten closer to the casket not ready to view her still. "Oh mama," she yelled.

"You don't have to go if you don't want to," her mother explained.

"I have to mama. I owe her that much." She leaned over talking to her baby as tears streamed onto Lasha's cheek. "I'll see you again. I love you." She started to feel hot and frustrated. "I love you." She started to show signs of another breakdown.

"I'm okay. Let me go Uncle Charles. Why did this happen?"

He grabbed her by the arm. "Come on baby," he said.

She snapped once she realized what Tamara had strolled into the funeral home wearing, a bright red pants suit surely wasn't what she had been instructed to wear today. A brand new, white and blue, two-piece dress sat on the back of her chair at Barbara's house. "*Red*" at a funeral was against fashion rules- a no-no.

"I can't believe she did this! Tamara you know what," Jeanette stormed towards her saying. She had gotten everyone's attention in room 101, 102 and 103.

"What's going on?" They all wondered.

"What are you talking about?"

"That's it Tamara," she took her hat off.

"What's wrong Jeanette?" asked Barbara.

She stepped into Tamara's face. "Why you didn't wear what I told you to wear? Are you trying to piss me off today? I bought you a white outfit."

"When have you ever seen me wear white? I don't like white, and I hate dresses! You should be glad that I came. You know how much I hate funerals."

She yelled. "This isn't about you!"

Walter whispered to his sister, "Only at our family affairs would you see shit like this."

She chuckled. "I know right."

"I know it's about that brat! She's dead and she still got you wrapped around her finger."

"You are a selfish bitch," said Jeanette, as she slapped Tamara hard across her face. A few concerned family members jumped up and ran over to them, including the funeral director. "What's going on?"

Diane quickly grabbed Tamara and pushed her outside as Barbara took Jeanette into the bathroom for a one-on-one talk with her. Tamara talked briefly with Diane dismissing every word; she promised to behave and angrily went back in, sitting in the corner alone. She took a seat in the back because she didn't want or need the nightmares from seeing Lasha.

After the situation was under control, the preacher asked Barbara to read a scripture. Reverend Smith read another scripture from the bible; Diane read the acknowledgments and obituary. Lexis and Lynette gave three-minute remarks about their niece. It was time for a song selection Diane shockingly said, "Performed by Tamara Brown."

"What? I'm not going up there."

"Go up there," commanded Barbara.

"What am I supposed to sing?"

"The eyes on the sparrow," she explained. "You know that song well."

She begged not to go in front of everyone.

"Will you do it for me?"

Tamara dragged her body from her seat and hesitatingly walked in front of the crowd. She closed her eyes as she tried blocking out the visions of being over her little sister's crib with the teddy bear in her hand. She panicked once she realized that her sister wasn't breathing, and that *she* had been the cause. **I had gone into the room to pick her up from crying. I didn't plan on hurting her, but something clicked when I couldn't stop her from crying. I blacked-out and when I came to she wasn't breathing. Something told me to do it; if I wanted my life back I had to do it. I can't tell anyone. I'll go to jail,** thought Tamara.

She felt the sweat trickling down her back. Everyone had their eyes locked on her as they waited for her to sing. Visions flashed of Lasha asking her, "Why did you do this to me?" It looked as though the casket was shaking as Lasha scratched on the inside crying, "Let me out! I want my mama!"

She couldn't do it; she ran off of the stage and into the bathroom. Barbara and Diane ran after her.

Reverend Smith (looking like a younger version of Jessie Jackson) stood at the pulpit as he performed the eulogy. He concluded the service by calling the pallbearers up to the front. "Let us pray. Bless this family, Oh Lord, in their time of need. Give them strength, Oh Lord to carry on because with you, all things are possible Father. In Jesus' name... we pray, amen."

"Amen," the people replied.

He signaled the four pallbearers to the casket. He started singing, "I'm going home to see My Father..."

The music started, and that automatically flicked on the switch of tears and sobbing as they closed the casket for the final time. The closing of the casket is the last call for being able to see our loved ones. In this lifetime, at least we hope.

Jeanette had stuck her hands into her pocketbook. "Forgive me Lord."

She pulled out a .25 semi-automatic pistol and aimed it directly at her head. Everyone screamed and ran towards the exit signs causing a loud, chaotic confusion in the little building.

"Oh my Goodness," They yelled, running out. "She's got a gun!"

Her immediate family went towards her to stop her, others thought, 'To Hell with that! I'm getting out of here!"

Charles pushed Barbara out of the way as he leaped at Jeanette's right arm. They tussled over the gun as it went off (he stopped her from blowing her brains out but didn't stop the bullets from escaping the gun. "I got it! What's wrong with you Jeanette?"

She stood there with a demented grin upon her face.

Tamara staggered towards her grandmother. "Grandma, I've been shot," she mumbled. She had her hand over her heart. I should not have worn this red outfit, Nia told me that it was bad luck," she laughed before she collapsed to her knees.

"Someone call an ambulance! Tamara's been shot!" Barbara yelled.

"What?" Jay asked.

Jeanette started laughing hysterically like a psychopath at those words.

"Ha, Ha, Ha! Let her die. Let her die! She's a murdererrrrrr. She killed my baby!"

She lost consciousness, although she was still able to hear the people as they yelled and screamed around her. The thunder struck outside the house causing Tamara to jump up in the middle of the bed as sweat poured down her body. Her pajamas felt like she had taken a shower in them. Her heart pounded a thousand times per second. She could not catch her breath.

"I was just dreaming," she touched her chest to verify that it was indeed a dream. "No gunshot wounds." She was relieved. She glanced at the clock; it was five fifteen in the morning.

"I'm not going to that funeral. I' m not going to get shot and Jeanette's been doing crazy shit lately too. I'm staying my black ass right here. Now what can I do to get out of going to this funeral but not make myself look like an insensitive bitch? I think I'm coming down with the flu. "Ha-choo."

She went into the bathroom and forced her fingers down her throat. She knew that Barbara was awake because she got up every morning around four o' clock.

"Are you alright in there?"

"No, I don't feel well. I have diarrhea and I'm throwing up. I think I caught the flu from Nikki's cousin." She smiled. "Grandma I feel like I'm about to die. I'm not going to the funeral today. I can't make it. I know Jeanette's going to be upset at me, {like I really give a damn.} but I don't think I can make it."

"If you're sick there's nothing that can be done about that. Drink plenty of fluids and stay in the bed. After the funeral, I'll nurse you back to health."

She said sickly, "Okay. My stomach hurts." She smiled. **Maybe a career as an actress wouldn't be too far-fetched because I'm good.** She was unable to go back to sleep because of her nightmare. It was obviously her conscience playing a major part of why she dreamed something crazy like that. "I know what I can do.......

Dear Diary,

I'd just experienced one of the craziest dreams ever. I went to Lasha's funeral and Jeanette got mad and slapped me because I had on a red pants suit. They tried to make me sing at the funeral in front of everyone. You know I hate crowds especially singing in front of them. Once they closed the casket, Jeanette tried to shoot herself in the head, but she shot me instead, right over my heart and then laughed about it. Uncle Charles told her what, she had done to me, and she called me a murderer and the word "murderer" echoed. Everything moved in slow motion after I got shot. I guess this is something that I'm going to have to deal with forever. I asked and pleaded with Jeanette to take Lasha over to her other grandma's house sometimes, but she refused to listen to me.

I must feel some type of guilt because I'm having dreams like this. Sometimes I care about what I've done, but most of the time I don't. I heard grandma mention that we should repent for our wrong doings. I think this qualifies as a bad sin, if any. I didn't want to go to the funeral in the first place, but after this dream, I'm definitely not going. I'm kind of glad that I dreamed that because it sparked a new plan for me. I can spend tomorrow on the phone talking to my new friend, Tyrese. Yes, it's the same boy that Nia's talking to. We went to the show the other day, and I enjoyed myself for the first time in months. He doesn't know that I'm Nia's friend. I don't know what I am to her. She's in love with this fool. I have to admit that he's cute, but I'm going to play this buster for whatever I can get out of him without putting it out, but there's a bonus to all this; Nia's going to hurt just like I did when she told the entire fifth grade school that I had a crush on Charles, and they teased me about it. Betrayal hurts worse than any wound you could get. It's been years and she's going to feel the sting from me. No matter how long it takes me to figure out your punishment. You cross me; there are no rules, no exceptions and no time limit. T.Brown

20 Months Later

May 29, 1993 (Saturday)
Diary Entry
Hello Diary,

It's a beautiful morning and I'd better enjoy it because this afternoon Jeanette will be home from the mental hospital. She did as well as what was expected of her at the funeral, (so I've heard) but two weeks later something snapped, causing her to have a nervous *breakdown*. She would talk to you one minute, throwing things at you the next for no apparent reason. You never knew what kind of mood she was going to be in, so when Damarcus' mother, Charisse, decided to file a missing person's report on him; she lost whatever little sense she had left. Her disdain for me began to show more and more. She told me a dozen times that she hated me and wished that I had died instead of Lasha. Grandma couldn't have moved in with us, but she asked me if I would be willing to stay home and keep an eye on her. I'm just a teenager, so what do I look like watching her? That's retarded? Nevertheless, I did it. Once she hid in the basement with a knife waiting to stab me that was my last straw. If I hadn't used my tray as a shield, she would've gutted me like a fish. I wasn't going to have to sleep with one eye-open or put chairs behind my door, so I moved back in with grandma.

The family visited her while she was in the hospital, but I wasn't thinking about her. Jeanette was convinced that I did something to her precious baby girl, *and whenever she mentioned it, I would ask her to prove it. Whatever small talk* we used to do was all gone now. She didn't speak to me, and I have no feelings or words to share with her. *I.HATE to even write about her in my diary let alone SPEAK to her.*

I have a new male friend, but I can't tell you who he is, he made me swear not to write about the things that we did at Jeanette's house. Charles hasn't talked to me because I didn't want him to be my boyfriend, that's when he looked for a new love. Two months later, the poor girl was pregnant. I barely escaped that sinking boat. Tyrese, Nia's old boyfriend and my new boyfriend-well, (that's what he thinks,) is taking me shopping today. She's not speaking to me either, because one of her nosey girlfriends went back and told her that she had seen me with her boyfriend. I had spotted her from the beginning and purposely went into her direction so that she *would* see us. We argued about it of course, but like I told her, "I didn't know that they were dating." (I'm a stinker. I know.) She couldn't prove that I had seen him when he picked her up from school that day. I'm far sighted☺ Maybe she will seriously think about it next time before she embarrasses someone who she claimed to be her best-friend. That incident haunted me for years, so maybe now I can put it all behind me.

"The Fight"

The family gathered at Barbara's house anxiously waiting for Diane to arrive with Jeanette. Barbara spent the entire morning in the kitchen cooking, as her brothers worked on the yard. Alexis and Lynette were responsible for the house chores, and she put her sisters on the grill. Tamara wasn't anywhere around like always.

It was hot as hell, but they were used to this kind of weather- they were from Alabama.

They had two reasons to celebrate: Jeanette was being released from the hospital and Diane and Marion's wedding was scheduled for next week. Diane wanted to share her final decisions with the family about the type of flowers she had chosen, and the picture of the cake.

About an hour later, a horn sounded. Everyone stopped what they were doing and ran to the car. Barbara instantly realized a change- a good change- in her sick daughter; she had gained weight and actually for the first time in months looked like the old Jeanette. The one before Lasha and Damarcus came into her life, heck the one before Tamara-the one that she had gotten along with- the innocent one.

Barbara patiently waited her turn (which was last), to hug Jeanette but she didn't mind. They finally stood there in a tight embrace, silently crying and laughing for at least a minute.

Diane said, "Mama you are going to- (she quickly caught the word suffocate, choosing to say,) "Let her go," she said laughing, making everyone laugh. While they were glad for her to be home; they walked on eggshells waiting for the "Crazy Jeanette," to appear.

They removed pictures of Lasha and Ashley-anything that could have sent them rushing her back to Northwest Mental Hospital.

Jeanette relaxed in the living room laughing and having a good time with her sisters talking about the good old days. The two dust filled fans that rotated in the middle of the floor hadn't supplied enough breeze for her, so she excused herself and went outside. The sisters exchanged concerned stares of worry with each other, telepathically thinking, "Is it starting?"

"It is cooler out here y'all, let's sit on the porch," she told them.

They exhaled collectively. "Okay," replied Diane. "Come on."

Outside provided a little more comfort than the house. The oven had been kicking out heat since seven thirty this morning, not to mention the house full of people roaming around.

Jeanette felt the tension in the air, but her doctor told her to expect that. It was an adjustment that the family had to endure. She was proud of the progress that she had made, even though she was aware that she had a long road to travel. But for the first time in sixteen months (without supervision of a doctor) she felt in total control of her thoughts and actions. She wasn't angry or sad and was enjoying being with her family.

The eighty nine degree, late evening weather brought about a group of kids who played in the middle of the street with the fire hydrant on full blast. They ran around loud-mouthed, and out of control like they owned the street. People who drove past blew their horns numerous times before they would let them pass.

Sixty-five percent of the Glenfield residents were outside shooting the breeze. The Kelly's were having a Sweet 16 birthday party for Shantanique, and there were no parking spaces available on the whole block. When Mr. Johnson's niece came to visit, she had to park around the corner. She fussed all the way to his house because she could never park in front of her uncle's house. Cynthia Parker sat on the porch watching her two daughters as they played tag. Betty Harris and her husband washed their cars in the backyard. Pookey; who did a little bit of everything, posed on the porch drinking and staring at neighbors, and polluting the air with their special kind of cigarettes. Music was always blasting from the house.

The new neighbor Tiffany, who lived directly across the street, relaxed on the side of her house. She enjoyed the shade while avoiding her neighbors, so she wouldn't have to speak to them.

Tiffany fussed at her children as they played in their pool in the front yard, splashing each other.

"Rumor has it is that she doesn't like black people. Mr. Love told Mrs. Brooks, who told Mr. Daniels, who told Angel Oliver, Mr. Love swore it to be true because she'd confided this bit of information to him as they were shopping last month at the grocery store. Although he didn't consider himself "gossipy", most *(if not all)* of the gossip that circulated on the street originated from him.

Jeanette laughed at her mother. "Ma, you know that you can't trust anything that Mr. Love says. You can tell him, "The sky is blue today," and it would get back that you said, "Some girl named Sky died yesterday."

"He can't hear," said a laughing Alexis.

"Perhaps he can't," Barbara said. "Or maybe he likes to keep shit started?"

"He's too old for that," Diane said.

"Well, if she did say that, it doesn't matter because she's no better than the rest of us, living in the same neighborhood, shopping at the same stores and every six months having an appointment at the ADC Office," Barbara explained.

Diane asked, "When are people going to stop being ignorant?"

"About a second before the world ends," Lynette answered. "So mama, if she was in trouble, and you were the only one around, would you help her?"

"Good question," Diane said.

"I bet it is," Jeanette laughed. "Sounds like A Diane Question."

"Leave me alone," Diane retorted.

Barbara paused for a minute thinking carefully before she had answered her question. "Yes, I would because I don't have to be ignorant because she is. I couldn't stand around and watch anyone die because of ignorance."

The *Real* reason why Tiffany had never spoken to any of them because she heard from Kim, who said that Mr. Harris told her that Mr. Love had said, that the Brown's didn't like her kind because her mother was a maid and had gotten killed by white folks, and she had better keep her distance from them if she knew what was good for her. I guess it never dawned on Tiffany as to how ridiculous that sounded; being that a white guy cut her grass every other week, and some white kids always visited her house to sell her candy to the family.

A prejudice person would not voluntarily give their money away to someone that they didn't like, and the fact that her mother was still alive made the rumor utterly absurd.

But they were not excused from the ignorant bug. Tiffany had dated and shared two of the four of her children with a black man. Even if she didn't share African American features, her great grandfather was as black as charcoal. If the people from the block had minded to their own affairs, they probably would have gotten along, or at least had spoken.

"I heard that she was a drunk, and she beats the hell out of her children for nothing."

"Mama, do you see how they act? I would beat their asses too, and I would become a drunk also," Lynette said. "I would hit the bottle hard---those four boys are terrible?"

"Y'all better get back in there and play before I make you take that pool back in the damn house. I'm not going to tell you again!" Tiffany felt their eyes piercing from across the street at her. "Look at them prejudice bastards?" she thought.

"Look at her abusive ass," Alexis said.

Jeanette sat on the bottom step checking out the scenery. Lynette had gone downstairs to get ready for work. She didn't want to go in and miss out, but she couldn't afford to call-off. Barbara decided to take a shower to cool off.

"I'll be back."

"Okay," Jeanette said.

Jeanette watched the two little boys who lived directly next door make an ant farm. They had filled the empty pickle jar with the dirt. "Put the ants in here!"

One of the boys looked up and waved to Jeanette. "Hi Alexis," Little Michael said, grinning.

Jeanette smiled and waved back. "I'm not Alexis. I'm her sister Jeanette."

"I'm Alexis." Alexis corrected.

"I thought that was Alexis," whispered Michael to his nephew.

He hit Michael with the stick. "You are stupid. Put the ants in here! She doesn't like you!"

"Told you that wasn't Alexis," said Daurel.

They argued back and forth without taking their eyes off the ants because they didn't want to get distracted from their project.

"They're making an ant farm," Alexis mumbled. **I remembered doing that when I was younger,** she thought to herself.

"Daurel, what are you about to do with those ants?" asked Diane.

Little Michael came from the back with a gasoline container in his hand. "We are about to pour this in the glass and burn them all."

"He's about to do what?" Barbara asked Jeanette, walking back onto the porch.

"Burn the ants up," Lexis answered chuckling.

"Little Michael and Daurel, you better not burn those ants up! And if I catch either one of you playing with gasoline or matches- I'm going to whip your asses *AND* then tell your mama! Do you two understand me?"

They nodded. Daurel said, "Man you talk too much. You should've stayed back there so we could've burned them. Stupid," he hit him upside his head.

"Don't call me stupid! You are stupid. You better stop hitting me!"

"You two have no business doing that to those ants. That's not right. Let them out," said Barbara.

"Aw man," said Daurel. He poured the ants out of the jar.

"She is not my mama," whispered Michael.

"You tell her that then," he mumbled.

"No!"

"So how are you feeling Jeanette?" Barbara asked.

She smiled. "I'm fine."

"Are you sure?"

"Yes ma, I was thinking about going back to school for nursing."

"Why wouldn't you?" asked Lynette.

"I think I'm too old."

"You're thirty four. It's never too late to learn," Diane replied.

"I know."

A Silver Honda wildly pulled up in front of the house with N.W.A booming from the speakers. "Who in the world is th-?" wondered Barbara.

"That's Tamara mama," explained Lexis.

"That's her," she whispered to Tyrese. He checked her out over his glasses. "Your mama is kind of cute."

"Whatever," she jumped out of the car with her hands full of bags.

All eyes were glued on her. She smacked her lips thinking**. Here's the crazy lady.** "Hey grandma," Tamara said.

"You don't see anyone else out here?" asked Diane.

"I see you went shopping girlie," said Barbara.

She looked over her sunglasses at them. "No one that I like much," she replied.

"Who was that?" asked Jeanette.

"Hello to you too Jeanette," she said sarcastically.

"Hello, who was that?"

"What's it to you?"

"Tamara," her grandmother yelled out.

Diane shook her head. Lynette thought, "**Great, just what we need Tamara.**"

"What grandma? I merely asked a simple question." She stood with her hands on her hip.

"What do you think I'm going to try and steal your boyfriend?" Jeanette playfully said. Tamara obviously wasn't in a joking mood because she swung her bags knocking her mother to her knees in the grass. Jeanette jumped to her feet and they started fighting like cats and dogs.

They were actually fighting like strangers, and it took all of them to pry them apart. It happened so fast no one was prepared even though they were standing right there.

Neighbors observed "The Crazy Fighting Family." Individuals pulled their vehicles over to the side to watch the ruckus. Barbara fought with Jeanette to free Tamara's neck from her hands as Diane had the hard task of getting Jeanette's hair untangled from Tamara's hands. Alexis tried to get Tamara's legs from being wrapped around Jeanette. It definitely was a family effort. William's car was parked in the backyard with the stereo blasting, so they were unaware of "The Fight." Once they had gotten them apart, Tamara wasn't done, attacking Jeanette again. Diane and Lynette had to drag Tamara's wild acting ass into the house.

Tamara tried breaking loose. "They should've kept her in that crazy house a little while longer! "Get your hands off of me!"

Barbara and Alexis stood outside talking to Jeanette. She seemed calm. She even started laughing. "I guess I can't play with her anymore? She's still mad at me."

Barbara laughed, trying to catch her breath. "I guess so."

Jeanette noticed blood dripping on her shirt. Her nose started to sting.

"She busted my nose."

"Pick those things up and take them in the house," Barbara told Alexis.

William finally came to the front. "Whose clothes are those on the ground?"

"Don't bring your ass up here now asking us damn questions!" Barbara exploded.

Diane and (a now calm) Tamara came from the backyard as Jeanette went into the house to clean her nose.

"Where are you going?"

"I'm taking her for a ride."

Tamara sat in the car looking out the window as her aunt gave her a long speech about respect. She just nodded to all the questions because she had heard it all before.

Diane went inside the store to buy band-aids for Tamara (her nail had broken down too far and was bleeding.) Tamara noticed a yellow folder over the sun-visor that was marked MY WEDDING. It contained the names and phone numbers of the businesses where she was planning on getting her wedding supplies from. There were pictures of the bridesmaid's dresses, the wedding cake, and brochures from the catering and photography companies.

"I should throw this folder underneath the car and there will be no wedding, and I won't be pressured into wearing a stupid ugly dress." Diane walked out of Perry Drugs. She quickly closed the folder and placed it back under the sun visor.

"We're going to have fun today," said Diane. "I know you are still upset with your mama-"

"Jeanette."

"She's better. Try and get along with her for mama's sake Tamara."

Yeah right, thought Tamara. "I'll try."

Dear Diary,

Today is Sunday May 31, 1993 and me, (my associate) Nikki, my cousins Caylen and Breonna were staying the weekend with the soon-to- be Turners. It's 4:19 am and everyone's asleep but me. Marion went to sleep about an hour ago watching television in his recliner. Actually, the television was watching him. He seems nervous about getting married, and if it wasn't for Diane pressuring him, it probably wouldn't have happened-not this week. I feel pressured to be a stupid bridesmaid, and they want me to sing with Charles. That's what we get for being on the side of the house playing (singing together) and grandma overheard us. We always challenged each other to see who knew the words to certain old school slow jams. That was one thing that, even after we stopped being special friends- we still did in the backyard. Grandma suggested to Diane that we sing in the wedding, so we had to rehearse and sing to her. I did not sing my best because where Charles doesn't mind singing in front of people- I do. He was in our school's choir and band, plus he was in his church's choir so this is a hobby for him. His girlfriend has a problem with him coming to practice for the wedding with me, but I'm here to tell her that,

I'm not the problem, he is. She needs to worry about her man and not me. With a baby coming soon, he won't have time or money to spend on me and I never double dip anyway. Diane obviously liked the way that we performed because in six days I will be standing in front of a room full of strangers. Friday, after the fight and after Diane and I had come back from the store, everyone was waiting on us to eat. Grandma gave me her usual speech about Jeanette, but it went in and out like it always does. Jeanette was trying to be sarcastic, and I know it. She had that devilish grin on her face. Even if she was playing, I don't have anything to say to her- let alone to be playing around like she didn't try and kill me. She can fool the doctors, pull the family's eyelids down over their eyes, and maybe even convert herself into thinking that she's changed, but she will never convince me. She's not a different person; I can see it in her eyes, she's as fucked up as before. Yes, I hit her first, but I owed her that from when she tried to stab me. Memories flooded my brain from that day in the kitchen, and I lost control of my hands. I have a few scratches on my back and neck from Diane trying to stop the fight. We will get our chance to duke it out like we both so desperately want to. Anyway, it seemed (from my room) that the family enjoyed themselves. I think they used this time to rehearse for the wedding and learned a few new "Hustle Dance Steps." I refused to mingle with Jeanette, and I wasn't going to get ate up by the mosquitoes, so I stayed on the phone with Tyrese and Nikki until the party was over. Marion took me to pick up Nikki, and we went to their house for the weekend. Saturday, we got dressed and went to the mall to pick up my silly looking dress. Caylen was upset because she wasn't asked to be in the wedding. Even though I don't care, I'm her niece so that's why I was asked first right? If everyone's in the wedding, who's going to watch Diane come down the aisle? Her sister didn't seem to be bothered by not being in the wedding, her only concern would be which way was the buffet table. Caylen is Aunt Louise's baby, and it shows because her lips stayed poked out and her attitude was revealed. You're not in the wedding little girl. Suck it up. One day you'll be in your own wedding so be quiet, and be thankful that you don't have to get up in front of all those people and sing. I must admit that I instigated the entire plan behind her being upset. I did it because it was necessary for what I had planned next. I told Caylen that I thought it was bold that she wasn't going to be in the wedding. And then I went to Diane and was like, "Look at Caylen pouting. She's mad at you because you didn't invite her to be in the wedding. She's such a baby." Both fell into my web. I hope that I can trust Nikki because she's going to be tested this week. I'll see how faithful she really is. I'm so tired of hearing the family talk about this wedding. I personally can't wait until it's done and over with. You should've seen the way that Diane looked when I made breakfast this morning. I don't know where Diane has been, but you don't let another woman cook breakfast for your man. She was always somewhere with her head stuck in a book. Don't get me wrong, nothing is wrong with learning. I read a lot also, but she should have taken some time to learn how to cook from grandma like I did. None of these young girls (family or not) would be over my house around my man. I gathered that some people never learn because if Aunt Max and Kelly wasn't an eye-opener for her, I don't know what else would be. I don't know if I should trust Nikki, especially since she said that the Bible considered it a sin if you fought your mother. Well, I guess I'm doomed to hell because if she hits me, I'm hitting her crazy ass back. That rule goes for whomever. I believe that from all my past experiences and definitely for my upcoming plans; I have a one way, front row ticket with my name on it, directly across from Lucifer himself. No, I don't think this is funny or cute, but I can't help the way that people make me react. From Jeanette's recent actions, "The apple doesn't fall far from the tree," cliché comes to mind. I can't wait to see my secret friend tomorrow. "Eventually, this is going to have to stop." My secret friend tells me but then he will turn around and page me with (07300116.) That's the code for me to call him which is our birthday months together. I'm just full of clichés today: "Why pay for the cow, when you can get the milk free?" We're not getting anything for free-if this secret comes out then we will *pay* for it dearly. I might have a couple of missing pages from you again after the wedding day. I'll write in you later. And explain things better.

Your friend, Tamara

Everything That Glitters Isn't Gold

This wedding could have been recorded in the Guinness Book of World Records for- the weirdest event- EVER. The morning started off with the bride coming on her menstrual cycle two-weeks ahead of schedule, (*There goes the honeymoon*)not to mention her comfort level in her white wedding dress (that she had no business wearing according to tradition) but that was the least of her concerns if she actually had any dress to wear at all.

She stood shocked in the middle of her huge walk-in closet, mouth to the floor looking at a previous dress that some sadistic, demonic dress shedder had gotten a hold of, leaving just enough dress to look like a belly shirt on the hook inside its plastic. She released a loud roar once the image registered to her brain, and it came through her mouth. The gang from last weekend ran into the room trying to help out a distraught bride-to-be in less than five hours (who happens to be dress-less in case anyone hasn't noticed.)

After the dust settled, Caylen had been accused of this horrendous act since she was mad that she wasn't in the wedding. No one could prove it, so it was just accusations. A hysterical Diane called her mother and soon after, Caylen used the phone in the kitchen and told her mother to come and rescue her. She pleaded her innocence crying, but that didn't help matters. Her sister assured her that she wasn't going to allow anyone to hit her. She told Diane, "You can think or say what you want, but no one is going to touch my sister. She's not the only person here! We don't know that Nikki girl, who's to say that she didn't do it?"

"Someone did it! My dress didn't rip by itself!" Diane screamed.

Tamara went into the closet only to retrieve a cut up lavender and white flowered dress. She carried the pieces of the dress to Diane almost causing her to have a heart attack.

Barbara arrived at the house within minutes of her call. She calmed Diane down first, and then took the girls into the kitchen to investigate, but no one told or knew who had become Miss Edward Scissor Hands. Diane couldn't figure out how or when Caylen, or whomever had the time to cut the dresses without anyone seeing them. It was a mystery indeed. Someone knew something; that was for sure. However, time wasn't on their side, and Barbara had to remove her nieces from the house before things got out of hand.

She took Tamara with her to get another dress. She would get the first dress that Diane had chosen before she had opted for the one that had been shredded. I guess she's forced to wear it now. Diane called the salesperson at the bridal shop and explained what had happened to her dress. She asked if she could somehow give her mother the original dress that she had chosen. They made plans on meeting at the church to get Diane ready no later than three o'clock. Doing all this last minute, unexpected, running around was going to be a challenge-most definitely.

Once they arrived at the church Barbara tried to reassure her distressed daughter that everything was going to work out right. That was before Lynette arrived at the church cake-less. The lady at Oaza Bakery had informed her that the groom had canceled the order for the cake two days ago saying that his sister was going to surprise the bride with a cake. That would have been nice, if any of his sisters could boil water correctly let alone make a three-layered wedding cake.

Lynette didn't see a reason to be alarmed until she got wind of the dress incident. She overheard her Aunt Ann telling Uncle Charles about the dress nightmare. She pulled her mother to the side and told her about the cake and Barb, in turn, called Marion at his brother's house. Now it was time to ring the alarm and loud. Marion hadn't been anywhere near Hamtramck, especially not canceling cake orders. She explained to him, what had happened to the dress and now the cake. Something was definitely going on here. He told Barbara (after he'd stopped laughing) that he would have his mother and sisters stop at the bakery and get three full sheet cakes. "They may not be layered cakes, but they will at least have cake to eat."

Barbara had decided that by keeping quiet to Diane about the latest prank would be the best choice, no reason in getting her any more upset than she already was. However, when Diane asked (and Barbara was sure she would, and soon) about whether the catering company, photographer and DJ had showed up yet, Barbara had to blow the lid because she didn't know what else to do (there was no sign of them yet.) Like any other bride would have done- she freaked out. A normal twelve year girl couldn't possibly be this evil and destroy a wedding like this. Diane remembered that her receipts were un-organized in the folder and Caylen was the only one who had touched the folder last weekend. She could've kicked herself in the ass because she had sent her outside to fetch it. And now her wedding day had turned into a story straight out of a Stephen King novel, and no one's to blame but herself. Someone else was helping her with this devilish plan because grown people don't even think this cleverly.

Diane sent her Uncle William outside to the car to get the folder. She called the companies from the list, arguing with a few of them, but the only good had come out of it was that the DJ was still able to make it. The catering company receptionist explained that someone had called three days ago and cancelled her order even though she was aware of losing her deposit. They arranged for the remaining balance to be mailed. Nevertheless, there was no way that all that food could have been prepared in time for the wedding. She had four other orders scheduled for today. The photographer had scheduled another appointment, so he wasn't going to be able to make it either.

"Okay, it's time to panic now," Diane cried to her mother. Barbara refused to let the prankster ruin her daughter's wedding. She had the people in the church running around the eastside buying stuff. Alexis and Lynette went to Perry Drugs for some film and liquor. Ann and Louise went to the supermarket to buy some canned vegetables and beverages. Charles and Jay went to the dollar store for the dinnerware and aluminum pans. William went to KFC to get some chicken and biscuits. {Yes, what is a party without chicken?}☺

Barbara explained to the pastor that she needed to use the kitchen to cook a few things. She anxiously paced around the church waiting on them to come back with the items. Diane decided to stay in the bride's room on the sofa talking to Jeanette (anything to keep her occupied.) Within the hour, Barbara had her workers in place cooking and placing things where they needed to be. When the organ started, and the guests stood up for the bride to walk down the aisle Barbara had her handkerchief wiping away the tears, smiling (at her beautiful daughter, and at the fact that the prankster didn't succeed.) The wedding couldn't have been any more beautiful than if they had planned it this way, except for the part when the jokester spiked the grape Kool-Aid with castor oil causing whoever drank it to run back and forth to the bathroom. Barbara was elated to hear the pastor say those famous five words. "You may now kiss your bride."

It was still eighty-nine degrees Fahrenheit outside after the reception was over with. It was a beautiful night to take a ride somewhere and let the sunroof down to cuddle and look up at the stars. Marion walked around the basement (where the reception was held) secretly distracted by a few things that he didn't want to discuss with his wife when she told him that he seemed distant.

"You've been acting different all day," Diane mumbled to him.

He snatched the gifts off of the table ignoring her, heading to the exit sign. She stood there like a statue.

"Can you help us?" He retorted.

He opened the trunk placing the gifts that Barbara had carried out to the car.

"Thank you, mama."

"Come on William. Grab those gifts over there and take it out," she ordered. "Let's get out of here," Barbara said. "My feet are crying."

"Diane, where do you want me to sit these plates of food," he asked.

"Um, sit them on the floor in the back seat, Uncle William."

Barbara hugged and kissed Diane. "Will you come by before you two leave for Hawaii?"

Diane looked at Marion, seeking an answer.

"Are we going to have time?"

"I guess so mama," he replied.

Barbara walked towards the raggedy blue car bare-foot. "Okay, I'll see you two later. Love y'all."

They said, "I love you too," in unison.

They waved, and drove away from the church, and you heard Barbara fussing at William. "I'll be glad when you get you another god damn car."

"Don't talk about my car, sis." He pinched her left leg. "That's how you get around so be quiet."

Diane stood in Marion's face with her lips puckered up trying to give him a kiss. "Where are we going Marion?"

"Home, where else are we supposed to go?" he snapped at her.

She attempted to put her arms around his waist, but he knocked her arms away walking back into the church.

"What's the matter with you honey?"

"Move," he said. He walked towards the church's side entrance door and locked it.

What did I do this time? She wondered. "Marion?" Why is he acting this way on our wedding day?

He kept walking. His heels continued clicking into the church's kitchen. He angrily tossed the empty aluminum pan that was left on the table into the garbage can forcefully. She wanted to go into the kitchen to help clean up, but she knew better to bother him when he was angry. She decided to go anyway.

"Honey," she said in a playful manner. "Baby cakes," she said, trying to soften him up.

"What Diane?" he exhaled deeply. "What do you want?"

She said smiling, "Can I hug you?"

He stood stiff as a board as she put her arms around him. "We are supposed to be celebrating today, not fighting."

He looked in Diane's eyes with this empty, beyond mad as hell look. "Move," he pushed her aside.

"Stop pushing me away from you."

"Well move then Diane," he explained carelessly.

"No, give me a kiss Marion." She tried to force him to kiss her. He grabbed her by the shoulders and threw her to the floor. "Is this what you want?" he asked wide-eyed.

"Let me go Marion! You're hurting me," she said with tears streaming from her eyes, trying to get up. He lifted her dress up ripping her pad and panties tossing them aside. He had this scary deranged look in his eyes. He grabbed her jawbone squeezing it with all his intoxicated strength.

"Please, don't do this here Marion." The more she begged for him to stop the harder and faster he humped. She closed her eyes and prayed for it to be over soon. *What if the pastor decided to come back to the church for something? This would be the most humiliating situation ever. How would she be able to look him in the face again? She hoped that GOD would send down a bolt of lightning and strike him in the ass as he humped on her like a dog.* After he had an orgasm, he kissed her neck and got up like he had done nothing wrong.

"Baby, look at my boxers and shirt," He stumbled fastening his pants. "I'm going to have to wash this before you take it back. Let's get out of here," he said, helping her up off the floor. "You got blood all over your dress," he said humorously. She walked out of the kitchen in a zombie-like-trance (no thoughts or words.)

"Will you make yourself useful," he asked, handing her the last six gifts off the table. He removed the brick from behind the door closing and locking it. She stood halfway into the hallway holding the gifts scared out of her mind not wanting to pass him.

"What are you standing there for?"

She took baby steps in his direction, with her hands full of gifts. As she walked halfway through the door, he let the door go, hitting her arm with it.

"Marion!" **Stupid ass!**

She pushed the door back opened using her foot. He opened the car door for her to place the gifts into the backseat. As she went to get out of the car, he pushed her into the backseat using his knee.

"Ride back there and lie down. And don't get any blood on my seats."

"Go to hell," she yelled. She quickly turned her head away from him.

She lay there crying, holding onto her stomach. He sped past Jane, Loretto, Filbert, and Wilfred streets within seconds it seemed. "You just raped me." She painfully moved onto her side. "Are you trying to kill me now?"

She just won't shut the fuck up talking to me, he thought.

"Slow down," she yelled, as she hit the back of the headrest. I wish I had my mace. I would spray him until his eyeballs fell out.

He looked at her from the rear view mirror still driving. "Don't make me pull this damn car over."

She sat up yelling. "Pull it over Rapist! Let me out!"

He quickly turned his head. "You're my wife. How can I rape you?"

"Rape is when a person forces another person to have sex against their will."

"Thank you, Webster Dictionary," he said with sarcasm.

"I said, "No"- and you kept doing it- and hard at that."

"You know you liked that as much as I did."

"No, I didn't, and to do this in a church? You are nasty because I'm on my period."

"When you're getting raped you yell for help." He continued saying, "I didn't hear you yell for help. I heard moaning."

"They were moans of aches and pains, not pleasure. Nothing was pleasurable about what you did to me." She exclaimed. "I'm sitting in a fucking car, bleeding with a wedding dress and no panties on, and I asked for this Marion? I'm enjoying this?"

"That's not what I saw. You need to live a little! We are married, we can fuck where ever we want to," he said amused.

She shook her head as many thoughts rushed in, but she couldn't find the right insult to match the silliest shit she had ever heard. He reached underneath the passenger's seat after he'd stopped at a red light and removed something from under the seat.

"What's this?"

He tossed a pink birth control package in the back seat at Diane. "I thought we were planning on having a child?"

"These aren't mine. It doesn't even have a sticker with the name of the person that it belongs to." She said, tossing the package back at him.

"You took the name off of it, in case I found it."

"It could very well belong to one of the girls. I'm not taking birth control pills. I swear!" she explained with a frightened look on her face. She thought that this might be a reason for another one of his beatings.

"Sure, just like you didn't ask permission from me before you went ahead and cut your hair."

"When did I ever ask you permission to do anything?" She rolled her eyes. "The last time I checked, I was an adult."

He pulled in front of their apartment. "You used to tell me everything before you did it, and now you think you can just make decisions like this before consulting me. What was the purpose of getting married?"

"Are you my fucking doctor or my damn husband?"

"What!" he said as he turned around and gave her a back handed slap to her face. It was so loud the people in the apartment building probably heard it. She placed her hand on her face and hauled off and punched him in the face with her right fist before she realized it.

"You son-of-a bitch," she attacked him from the backseat.

"Don't you ever hit me again!" he said, grabbing her hands squeezing them hard. "Bitch, if you put your damn hands on me! I'll kill you. Get out of my car!"

"Make me."

He tried pushing her out of the car. "You need to go in the house Bloody Mary!"

She spat on him, opened the door, and ran towards the apartment. "You crazy bitch!"

Mrs. Harrison, the old lady who lived on the third floor turned on the light looking down at them from the balcony. "Diane, are you alright?"

"See what you have done," she mumbled. He had her by the arm.

"Yes, I'm alright- we're just playing. Let me go," she whispered.

"Okay," she said heading back into her apartment.

"Fuck that old ass lady. She's too fucking nosey. I'm going into the house."

Diane went into the apartment and headed straight for the bathroom locking the door. **She flashed back to the first time Marion had grabbed her face because she playfully told him to be quiet. All this started after he fell and injured his knee and could no longer play football. He promised that he wasn't going to hit her again. But he had. She knew he was cheating on her but she didn't have concrete proof. What am I going to do? I love him, but I can't continue like this. I can't call and talk to mama because she would kill him with her bare hands.**

He had told her on quite a few occasions that she would never find another man who could love her the way he did and that no one else would want her but him." You can't satisfy me in bed like you used to." He told her. "It's your fault if I did cheat. Do you think another man will want you? Do you know how many women would love to be in your shoes?" He filled her head with this nonsense so often that she had started to actually believe it herself.

She got out of the shower and went into the bedroom to get her pajamas. He had stretched across the bed in the nude crying softly to himself. She wanted to just walk past him and let him suffer for a change, but she couldn't. "What's the matter with you Marion?"

"Come here, please- I promise I won't hit you." He sat up and hugged her.

"Diane, I have a problem, and I don't know what to do about it. My hopes of being a pro football player are over. I just wanted to give you a good life baby. I'm stuck working at Domino's for another three months until hopefully I can land a job at this software company. The bills are stacking up quicker than my little checks can pay for them."

She grabbed his hand. "I told you to let me help you with the bills, but you won't let me. I make good money."

"That's the problem, I'm the man and I'm supposed to take care of you; not you take care of me."

She kneeled down beside him. "Marion, I found the liquor bottles that you had hidden underneath the dresser. You're drinking too much and that's contributing to your violent behavior. Do you love me?"

He wiped his face, nodding. "You know I do."

"These last six months have been hell for me. You have hit me at least three times and you always come back and say that you're sorry, not to mention you've threatened to kill me if I leave. You're one way around the family, but you're another way at home and I'm becoming afraid of you. I'd rather you kill me from trying to leave than for me to live in fear of you. Both of us have tempers and I can't promise you that I will always be this calm and take this abuse from you. One of us is going to end up dead, and I love life as much as you do." She got up and went into the closet to get two comforters. He watched her walk away.

"Where are you going?"

"To watch television in the living room," but she really had plans on locking herself in the bathroom, just in case he started tripping again. He laid there completely naked, drifting off to sleep, letting the cool breeze from the fan hit his body.

Diane opened up the window, placed the covers in the bathtub and cried herself to sleep. She thought **about jumping in the car and going over to Jeanette's house, but she pictured him waking up in the middle of the night and waiting in the living room chair with a belt as she crept back into the house. I can't leave him now; he needs me.** She thought.

MISSING PAGES
THESE- R- MY- CONFESSIONS

Dear Diary,

Today is June 20th, 1993. It's Friday, around 10:45p.m, the last time I checked. I'm lying in bed watching television at my grandma's house (now home again) in my panties and bra because it's humid outside. It was one hundred and one degrees today, and now its eighty-eight degrees outside, not much better. I'm upstairs in my room (which is really an attic that had been converted into a bedroom) burning the hell up. My fan is on but it's blowing hot air on my body. I took three cold showers today to no avail because I'm sticky and sweaty again once I come back up to my room. I've been feeling sick since a week before the wedding. I hate to think about the wedding. That was a total waste of my time because everything that I planned failed miserably. Thanks to Grandma for saving the damn day. Well, I told you that I had a big secret to tell you so here it goes. The week before the wedding when I spent the night over at Diane's house, Nikki and I stole Marion's car and went to the store because I needed some cigarettes. I was more interested in being in the car, so I could jot down some information (You know the names and numbers of the businesses where she was going to get the stuff for the wedding.) The following morning, (at seven o'clock) Nikki and I walked to Damman's Hardware and had copies of the apartment keys made before anyone got up. Diane made it easy by laying her keys on the kitchen counter for me. We left and returned before anyone noticed that we had gone. They probably would've slept longer, but the smell of breakfast woke them up. That Sunday morning, Diane asked me to go and get the folder out of her car; I didn't want to put my hands on that folder under any circumstances, so Diane had Caylen go out to the car. I really didn't feel like going for one, but that helped for what I had planned. I was framing my little cousin to take the fall? Yes, I don't like her, and I always get blamed for everything, so now it was someone else' turn. She was showing us the pictures of the tuxedoes and flowers. I saw the receipt and immediately got a brilliant idea on what to do next. Diane put the folder in the top drawer in her room. I know because as I was coming out of the bathroom, I saw where she put it from the reflection on the mirror on her dresser. That Monday, Nikki drove her mother's car over to grandma's house and asked me in front of everyone if I wanted to go to the mall with her. She wanted to go shopping for a dress to wear to the wedding. {Yeah right?} We went straight to Diane's apartment while they were at work and school and I entered the apartment through the back door so no one could see me. It seemed as if that old lady from upstairs was always looking out of her window with her nosey ass. They didn't need a neighborhood watch as long as she lived there. I took the receipts from the folder and went to the corner store and made copies of all of them before returning them when I finished. We then drove to the west side and picked up Nikki's cousin David, so he could go inside the bakery and get a refund and cancel the order for the cake. He told the lady behind the counter that he was Marion. Diane was at work and he wanted to surprise her because his sister was a baker and she wanted to bake the cake for them. He let her see the copied receipt and Sally gave him the money without any hesitation. Of course, Nikki and I were nowhere around the bakery. We go in there all the time. We didn't even park the car on the same block as the bakery. He received fifty dollars for his services. Nikki received fifty dollars because she was his agent and I received one hundred and ten dollars because I was the mastermind and because that's what I said I was going to get. We dropped him off at home and we used a payphone on W. Eight Mile Road and Burt Road near a Popeye's Chicken restaurant. Nikki called, posing as Diane and cancelled the photography appointment. Kim told us to come and get the money, but we told her that we were too busy and we would be up there after the wedding. Then, we called the DJ and cancelled the music, but when it came time to cancel the food service, this nasty ass bitch of a receptionist got an attitude with Nikki. She was talking about their time is valuable and Diane shouldn't have had them schedule this day. That bit-. That lady was very unprofessional. I wanted to get on the phone and cuss her out myself, but I had to stay out of it. When you're guilty keep your hands clean. She asked for the number on the receipt and the time the service was scheduled for. She asked a lot of questions before she went ahead and cancelled it. My favorite part of all was Friday morning. I took the bus and went over to the apartment by myself and went into Diane's closet. I had a razor blade that I kept underneath my tongue sometimes, (I planned on using that) but I came across a pair of scissors in the closet. I tried on her dress before I shredded it. I thought I looked better in it than she did and I started cutting myself out of it. I didn't cut up my dress until four o'clock Saturday morning when everyone was knocked out because I figured she was going to ask me to try it on again for her and she did just that. I'm glad that I followed my first mind and waited. I put the scissors under the spot where Caylen was sleeping to set her up like the fool that she is. I played them both like a guitar and neither one of them saw what I was doing. Men aren't the only ones that are stupid. Case in point: Why did I do it- you should be wondering to yourself? Good question. I wanted to get back at Caylen and her sister for reading my diary three months ago (they didn't get to read much but still) Caylen was my target. Diane kept on bugging me to be in the wedding and to sing for her so I planned on fixing her for the unnecessary pressure that she put on me. If I said that I didn't want to do it- Leave me alone. I have other reasons that I don't want to elaborate on right now. The shit just didn't go the way I planned it. She got three free cakes from Sally. The DJ came after all. Grandma took care of the food situation. Marion reimbursed grandma for purchasing Diane's dress and grandma bought me a new one. Where did this lady have all this money stashed? After all that trouble, Charles and I still had to sing, I still had to wear a stupid dress even though I did look good and my boy Marion still got married. I was mad because Diane sat on me when Jeanette and I were engaged in "The Fight," that was my chance to kick her ass for slapping me a while back at grandma's house but Diane kept grabbing me. Think about it? What reason would I be hanging around Diane for? Something had to be very interesting for me to spend the weekend away from home. Lesson one: Never let females spend the night at your house and you have a boyfriend whether he's fine or not. Lesson two: Never let another girl prepare a meal for your man, especially if you can't cook. I'd caught him looking at my ass a few times, so she better be careful and learn some street smarts. You should be book smart, as well as street smart. To me, I think a street smart person is more valuable because you can work the streets to make money, while the book smart person is at home reading books, getting A's while their man is out screwing around on them. I've failed to mention that I'm five months pregnant. I feel like a big, hot mama whale. Jeanette mentioned to grandma about registering me in this center that's on a farm for troubled, pregnant teenagers. That's a bunch of B.S but I'll be leaving next week. I don't even care anymore. Who's the daddy? **I'll tell you some other time. Write in you later.**

DIARY ENTRY 9

Dear Diary,

Loving Center my fat, yellow ass! Nothing's loving about this f------ place. Yesterday was one of the worst days of my life. I realized for the first time last night that I will spend my 17th birthday in this damn prison. It's a nice, clean looking center, but it's nothing but a fancy girls' home. I knew that Jeanette was going to find some reason to do something stupid to pay me back, and because I had gotten pregnant, that was her chance to get rid of me. I haven't spoken three smart words to Jeanette since the fight so how am I a troubled-teen? I was good enough to watch her baby, but I'm a problem because I'm having my own child? Grandma allowing her to do this to me was the most shocking thing about the situation. She didn't stand up for me like I thought she would have. I've never been literally stabbed in the back before, but I can say I've experienced the closest feeling to it. I thought I was fucked up when Nia told everyone in school about my crush on Charles. That doesn't compare to the hurt and feelings of betrayal that I am dealing with now. It's like she's been brainwashed by Jeanette. Grandma is so intent on maintaining a good relationship with Jeanette that she doesn't care about messing up the relationship that she and I once shared. Normally, when I got mad, I sought revenge on the person who hurt me, but it's different this time. I could never hurt my grandma no matter what she has done to me, now this is truly a first for me. I'm mad as hell with her, but I can look in my grandma's eyes and see that she's hurting too. She's just caught in the middle of our war. I wanted to talk to her, but my pride wouldn't allow it. I never had regretted anything I've done in my life until yesterday, when I snatched away from her. As for Jeanette, I could rip her head off her body with my bare hands and not think twice about it. I could feel the vibes of hate coming off of her body. She tolerates me, but she doesn't love me, and I would put my life on that. I'm in a room by myself for now said Miss Williams (the lady runs this place) but not for long. This woman wobbles around the center like she's

GOD Almighty. She doesn't like or trusts me, and I don't like Miss Piggy either. I'm scheduled for my first prenatal visit tomorrow with Dr. Shavers at four thirty after class. Everything is scheduled by your last name and what grade you are in. I'm a sophomore right now. Thanks to Jeanette I will have a memorable birthday. Yesterday, I called Nikki, Charles and Tyrese and hollered at them for a minute. This place is so confining and you must present your ID card everywhere you go. We get three free passes per week to use the phones and we earn extra passes by getting good grades. There are security guards for every motherfucking (sorry) thing that we do in this place. I never talked on the phone much, but I had the freedom to pick up the phone if and when I wanted to. I guess you never miss a privilege until it's stripped from you. We even have scheduled times to shower and eat (sound like prison rules to me.) The shower rule was recently enforced to cut down on so much sexual activity. The next step was going to be that the guards were going to have to stand in there while we shower, but they are trying to avoid that one. They might as well; they are everywhere else anyway. Jeanette will pay dearly for this stunt that she pulled on me. The only good thing about being here I have access to some things that I need for an important mission that will possibly take me years to accomplish. Plus there's no sense of crying like a baby, so I'm going to make the best out of this unfortunate living arrangement that Jeanette has so cleverly planned for me. At least we have air-conditioning☒. Anyway; we eat breakfast at seven o' clock and lunch at twelve thirty and dinner at six in the evening. We must wear uniforms to school, but we can dress down afterwards. When the time came for me to take my ID photo, I kept on sticking out my tongue and sticking up my middle finger at the camera lady. The assistant called her master and told on me like I was about to get a whooping or something. Miss Williams told her to take the picture anyway. They want to see a troubled-teen so I guess a troubled-pregnant teen is what they are going to get. They placed the girls into classes based on a behavior scale of one through five. I'm a four so they say. I don't know where they got their information from but I'll have to do something about that classification. When Miss Williams left me in the room yesterday (during orientation) I used a safety pin and looked through her files and found a couple of interesting girls that need to be on my team so we can raise some hell in this loving center.

Mia Burns, Yasmine Colvin, Tracey King and Randie Davidson were the four girls who were classified in a group of their own. They weren't a five (they were a six), based on the fact that their folders were separate from everyone else's. Mia and Yasmine are eleventh graders in my math class while Tracey and Randie are in my English class. I picked the pharmacy course as an elective class so I could learn something new. You know I am always down to learn "new things". The lights are off for the night. We can't have television sets in our rooms, another stupid rule, so I'm about to listen to the music until I fall asleep.

Write in you soon.
Miss Brown

You Must Learn How To Adjust

(Saturday) August 29, 1993

The morning looked like it was going to be another beautiful day in Saginaw, Michigan. Tamara had decided around four this morning that she was going to pass on the "milking of the cow experience" for today's special project. It was hard enough to get back up once she sat down with her stomach being a nuisance. She was huge for six months and that stopped her every weekend from going outside with the rest of the girls on the farm. There was no way that she was going to kneel down on the side of a cow and try to milk it. If she wanted nasty milk, she'd might as well squeeze it from her own breasts and drink it.

She looked out of her window at the laughing (cow milking mamas) or pregnant hyenas. Everyone there wasn't pregnant, but 75% of them were, or had been before, including Randie, whose only sexual encounter with a male resulted in pregnancy. Her family was Catholic and abortion was out of the question. She was shipped to The Loving Center for three reasons: she was pregnant and a lesbian and the family was ashamed. This place must've been heaven sent because she's been here for three years without any hope of graduating anytime soon. This center isn't free, so she's milking her parent's pockets as well as some of the bi-sexual girls (not to mention the cows too.) She's enjoying every minute of this place.

Tamara watched the horses run around the track a few times wishing that she was one of them, but soon realized that they were just as trapped as she was. However, she had a release date, and they didn't. She sat in the middle of the bed writing a letter to Tyrese. She never had explained to him that she was six months pregnant, and he was the father (which he wasn't.) She wrote the address and directions to the center along with the days and times that she could have visitors. It was a three-hour drive, but she knew that he was going to come. She wrote to Nikki telling her to catch a ride with him along with a list of things that she needed from her. She hated the fact that she had to trust her with her man, but it had to be done. "Don't let me down Nikki," she wrote in her letter. She wrote a letter to Charles explaining to him that she was pregnant and the baby daddy was nowhere around and she was scared and needed a friend along with a list of things she needed him to bring to her like pajamas, panties, etc. She didn't care that he had a new girlfriend or a child. She had him wrapped like a fly in a spider web. She didn't know who fathered her child, but the baby was hers for sure. The stretching of her stomach and the (Bruce Lee) kicking baby proved that much. She had a pretty good idea who it was, but she wasn't going to worry about it right now.

Last week Jeanette, Lynette and Alexis wasted their free time trying to visit her just to get rejected. She would've gone down to chat with her aunts, but once she heard the name Jeanette, she turned around and refused to see any of them after a two-hour wait and three-hour drive. Alexis was heated and Lynette was indifferent about the situation, but Jeanette had expected it from her, that's why she told them not to mention her name, but they had to.

A few days later Barbara left a message for Tamara to call so they could have a talk about what she had done. She never called back because there was nothing to discuss. She did, however, write a letter to her grandma with the words written huge on the paper: NEXT TIME they'd better GET MY PERMISSION BEFORE THEY COME HERE, LOVE

YOUR FORMER GRANDDAUGHTER,
TAMARA.

The alarm sounded for the girls in buildings A through H to get ready for breakfast. Tamara had quickly gathered her belongings, practically running into the showers before everyone else came in. She always tried to be at least the second person in the shower to avoid bumping into Mia Burns, the center's pregnant bully who made it her business to tell anyone within earshot that the owner was her Aunt. She would pick on people and get away with it because of her special privileges. This was going to be a challenge for Tamara but that kept her on your toes. She was bound to come up with something. She always did and she was going to show Mia how to get and use special privileges.

There was a note on the door.

Reminder: 8:00 a.m. Ultrasound appointment for T. Brown with Dr. Shavers

In addition, new roommate Tina Young arrives at 5:00 p.m.

Tamara had her usual altercation with Mia today like most mornings. The girl with whom she wanted to conspire with had other plans, which didn't include Tamara. In fact, she didn't hide the harsh feelings that she had against Tamara.

Today, from her table she shot spitballs at Tamara causing her to want to smash her face in, but she refrained. She had a calculated plan for her, and she wasn't going to let her mess it up for her. She planned to unleash the demons on her and make the bitch beg for mercy. She switched tables and sat next to Randie and Tracey. After breakfast when Tamara strode past Mia, she stuck her foot out and almost made her fall. Mia's flunkies who sat at the table with her had all started to snicker and laugh. Tamara started to smack her with the tray, but caught herself, and they had a stare down for a minute.

"If you feel froggish, then leap bitch!" Mia said, inviting Tamara to make the first move.

Tamara kept on walking, counting to herself. The auditorium filled with sudden laughter, and everyone went back to what they were doing. She looked back at Mia counting to ten and took in quick deep breaths as she sat the tray on the counter. She thought, Laugh now sweetie... You will be crying later. I promise you that.

"I'll kick her ass for you right now Mara," Tracy said, getting out of her chair. Tamara grabbed her arm. "Nah, don't worry about it,"

"I'll cut that bitch's head clean off her neck," added Randie. "I'll go to jail; I don't have anything to lose!"

"No," she insisted with a grin on her face. "I'm a reformed girl. I have other shit to deal with right now, but thanks for the concern ladies. I don't believe in being violent." **She doesn't want to join me, so I'll break her down to her knees.** Tamara took the last sip of her orange juice.

"Where are you about to go next?" asked Tracy.

"I have an appointment with Doctor Shavers," explained Tamara.

"Are you going to the Rec room later?" asked Randie.

Tamara replied, "How much money are y'all playing for?"

"Five dollars," replied Tracey.

"I can guess I can take y'all money," Tamara said laughing.

"Bet," said Tracey.

"Later," said Tamara.

Tamara rose from the table and Mia slithered out behind her. She pushed the elevator button going up. Mia bumped her hard calling her a bitch as she headed towards the stairs. **She's afraid of the elevators**, Tamara realized. She decided to take the stairs because the elevator took too long. As she went into the stairwell, she heard Mia walking heavy like her feet weighed a ton. Tamara pictured **Mia tripping her in the hallway the other day. Everyone thinks that I am scared of you so now I can do my thing. Payback is a mother. She thought back to the time when she walked into one of the bathroom stalls, and it read on the wall:**

FOR A GOOD TIME LADIES ASK FOR TAMARA.
ROOM 123- from M.B

Inside Dr. Shavers' office

Tamara lay shivering on top of the examination table with her hands resting across her chest as her thigh was exposed. "I'm cold Dr. Shavers."

"I'll be done shortly Tamara."

Dr. Shavers typed some information into the ultrasound machine. Tamara didn't know what to expect of this machine, so she nervously asked, "Is this procedure going to hurt?"

She chuckled. "Not at all," she giggled. "I will squeeze some gel onto your stomach, and I will use this instrument here," she showed her the handle used to see the baby. "I will place this onto your stomach, and I'll be able to take pictures of the baby. Totally painless, just trust me."

You're a doctor and I don't trust doctors, she thought as Dr. Shavers lifted the hospital gown so she could place the gel onto her stomach.

"You're not kidding," she said laughing. "It is cold."

Dr. Shavers moved this instrument across her stomach as she looked at the monitor. "Oh my," she said as a look of concern crossed her face.

Tamara jumped up. "What's wrong with my baby?"

"Lay back down Tamara."

She bounced back up. "No, what's wrong with my baby?"

"I'll be right back," said Dr. Shavers. She snatched Tamara's chart of the table and dashed out of the door. She sat up staring at a blank monitor. "What in the hell is going on with my baby?"

Dr. Shavers banged on Miss Williams's door like someone was after her.

What now? I'm trying to eat," thought Miss Williams. "Come in," Miss Williams roared out. **Damn it!** Dr. Shavers came into the office looking as though she had just caught a glimpse of a poltergeist. "We have a problem Sharnita."

Miss Williams took a bite out of her turkey and egg sandwich. "What now Wendy?"

"I was giving an ultrasound to Tamara Brown from room 12."

"I know her…and?"

She tossed her chart onto the table. "Look at page nine."

She took one last bite of the sandwich wiping her hands on a napkin. "I don't know what I'm looking at," she explained as she put her glasses on.

"I gave Tamara an ultrasound, and I found an error."

"Stop beating around the bush and tell me what's going on," she declared. **I'm starving**, she thought.

The doctor walked in front of the desk pointing to the chart. "This is not right."

Miss Williams looked closer at the document. "What should it be? What she's not pregnant?"

"Yes, she is but there's a problem."

"What is it? Damn it!"

She pointed to the document again. "Look here, and here."

"You're fucking kidding me right?"

"No ma'am."

Miss Williams looked incensed at her newly acquired information. "You're her doctor and you mean to tell me that you never discovered this problem before?"

She collected the papers and placed the clip back on the folder. "Dr. Bell had seen her for the first three visits because I was sick. The last visit, I was going to take her, but I was backed up, so she offered to take some of the patients off my hands with Tamara being one of those patients."

"How long have you been a doctor Wendy?"

She held her head down like her mother was scolding her. "Eight years."

"One more screw up like this, you will be out of here Wendy," she said calmly.

"I'm a doctor, but I make mistakes too. This was the first time that I'd seen Tamara as a patient."

She threw her sandwich into the garbage. "I don't pay you, as well as I do for mistakes Mrs. Shavers. In this business there are no room for mistakes."

"I informed you as soon as I noticed it myself."

"You should have noticed it before today. Just because you were absent, is not a good enough excuse for me. It was your job to look over all your patients' files to make sure that everything was okay.

"It's all Dr. Bell's fault. She could've told me."

"It's always easier to blame someone else," she giggled. "That wasn't Dr. Bell's patient, so she really didn't care. She wasn't getting paid to see her, you are." Miss Williams flipped through her Rolodex for Jeanette's number. "You're excused."

"What am I supposed to tell her?"

"Be creative, but don't let her know."

Dr. Shavers grabbed the clipboard off of the desk and left the room as Miss Williams picked up the phone and began dialing.

"Hello, may I speak to Jeanette," asked Miss Williams.

"This is she."

Back in the examination room

Tamara sat in the middle of the table swinging her feet back and forth. "Are you going to tell me what is wrong with my baby?"

Dr. Shavers strolled into the room with another ultrasound machine. "Relax Tamara. I'd discovered that there was a malfunction with my machine, so I have to give you another one with this. The images from this machine were showing that your baby didn't have a kidney and that freaked me out. Lay down Tamara."

She performed another ultrasound with the new machine. "There. That's better. You're having a healthy baby girl. Are your parents or another family member going to adopt the baby?"

"Adopt? I'm keeping my own baby."

"Okay, you can get up and put your clothes back on. We're done here."

"Doctor Shavers."

"Yes."

"Who would I talk to if I wanted to make a complaint?"

"About what?"

She started biting her nails telling her, "I fear for my life."

"Who do u fear?"

She paused. "Mia Burns."

The doctor stopped writing. "You mean Miss Williams' niece?" **Oh shoot**, she thought.

"Yes, she constantly pushes and throws spitballs at me, and yesterday she almost made me fall down the stairs. She placed a knife up to my throat and told me that if I ever told on her, she would kill me."

"Oh no, that type of stuff is not acceptable here. I will talk to Miss Williams for you, and you should leave a complaint in her box at the security guard's desk."

She smacked her lips. "I've already done that four times."

"Four times?" She said puzzled, "Do it again."

"Thanks doc."

"I'll see you in two weeks Miss Brown." She passed Tamara another bottle of prenatal vitamins and some pamphlets about the physical changes that an expectant mother will experience in their final months before delivery.

"She told me that she's her niece, and she can do whatever she wants to whoever she wants to do it to."

"I'm about to see her next, do you want me to talk to her for you?"

"Oh no, please don't say anything to her. She'll surely come back for me if you say anything. Let Miss Williams handle it. Please don't mention it to her Dr. Shavers."

"I won't, I promise."

She walked out of the office smirking.

What Goes Up Must Come Down

Tamara sat on the third level stairwell thinking about Mia and how she was going to handle her problem. She had written another complaint to Miss Williams and made a copy of the letter in the library before giving it to one of the security guards.

"Can you make sure that she gets this letter please?"

"I always do," she said not really caring if Miss Williams received the letter or not.

Tamara sat on the stairs eating a candy bar that she remembered that she had stashed in her purse. "Mrs. Shavers works for the pig so why would she piss her off for my sake?" she mumbled to herself. **I'm going to try and reason with her one last time**, she figured laughing. The door had squeaked and Tamara stood up walking down the stairs slowly. There were two girls who she had recognized but didn't know their names. They spoke and kept on about their business. She turned around and sat back down on the steps once they were out of sight. The door opened, and she eyeballed to see who was coming before she walked down. "Hey girl," said her science classmate.

"Hey," she said as she walked slowly down the stairs.

"Where are you wobbling too?"

"To the Recreation Room," she went through the door on the second floor, but turned around and went back onto the stairs once she was gone. "I am about to die if I have to keep on doing all this damn walking up and down these stairs." She gazed at her watch again. I'd been sitting on these steps for forty-five minutes waiting for this bitch," she mumbled. "What in the fuck is Dr. Shavers doing? Delivering her baby?" The door opened again and Tamara reluctantly stood up.

"I'll be up here later," said the girl.

That's her. That's Mia's voice," Tamara thought listening. She walked slowly, verifying that it was indeed Mia. "Yes, that's her bitch ass voice," she said underneath her breath.

Mia said, "Hurry up. Fat girl," she laughed.

Tamara turned around looking at her with this expression on her face that made Mia feel frightened.

"Move girl," She nudged Tamara with her elbow. "You're walking too damn slow and close to me."

She tried to brush past Tamara quickly because she felt in her bones that something was different about her today.

"Excuse you," Tamara yelled as she stuck her arm out to prevent her from passing. "Don't storm past me."

She pushed Tamara's arm out of the way. Tamara quickly scanned the premises like the terminator to make sure that no one was around.

"Wait a minute," Tamara angrily retorted.

She hurriedly walked down the stairs in front of her. "That's it," replied Mia. She made an attempt to push Tamara, but she took hold of her arm instead. Their arms were intertwined, as they scuffled either one not wanting to fall down the steps. Tamara snatched away and looked down at her bleeding arms.

"You scratched me." Tamara had allowed her to walk past her.

"You better be glad that was all I did to you," she said with a grin on her face that didn't last too long because Tamara sprinted at her, shoving her hard backwards over the second level floor bannister.

"KA BOOM," was the sound you heard as her body landed face down onto the first floor stairs.

"Help me," she mumbled. Tamara quickly proceeded down the stairs before someone interrupted their fun party. She kneeled down and untied her right shoelace so slickly that Mia didn't notice what she had done. She made an effort to get up, but Tamara forcefully stepped across her pregnant back. "Where are you going Miss Burns?"

People heard the loud crash but being in the stairwell, the sound was muffled and everyone carried on and didn't think to check there.

"Help me. I'm hurting," she said with blood flowing from her nose.

She smiled. "Well, Mia, that was my plan." She kneeled down so that Mia could see her face. "To hurt you," she whispered into her ear. "You've hurt me so many times. Look at what you have done to my arms bitch."

"I'm sorry," she cried.

She stood over her and stepped onto her fingers. She moaned out. Tamara said, "Oops. Sorry about that. Turn over," she said. "If we were up there and we were struggling. Your body would've landed this way once you fell," she grinned. She couldn't move because her ribs were fractured so Tamara turned her over.

"Please go for help," she pleaded with Tamara.

"You've messed with the wrong bitch this time Mia. I tried to get you to join forces with me, but no. What did you tell me in front of everyone? I don't need you. Remember that, I should just let you bleed until someone comes and finds you."

"No, please help me Tamara," she whispered.

She joyfully wrapped her hands around her throat laughing. "I could take your life right now!" But she decided against it. Mia gasped for air. "Oh, I'm Tamara now, but earlier I was a bitch. I thought I was the one that was unstable. Next time you touch me or even look at me crooked I will cut your eyeballs out of your head. I've killed before and I won't hesitate to do it again. If you mention my name to anyone I will be back and next time you won't survive. I promise you that and I keep my promises too." She kicked her (not hard but not necessarily soft) in her pregnant belly as she stepped across her to get out of the door. "Help, please help me," Tamara said mocking her and laughing as she exited through the door.

"Mia needs a doctor on the first floor!" She yelled to Ms. Woods holding onto her stomach. "Call Dr. Shavers," she hollered.

Ms. Woods asked, "What happened to you?"

"Mia tried to push me down the stairs on the third floor and both of us fell. Look at my arms?" She started crying. "I tried to grab her, but she fell anyway."

Dr. Woods hugged Tamara. "It's going to be alright. You need to be checked out."

"I only fell onto my knees."

"You still need to be checked out okay," she told her, "I'll call Dr. Shavers and see if she can check you out."

"Sure, but I'm fine. I just hope that she's okay," she said as she wiped her fake tears. "I knew something like this was going to happen."

Mrs. Woods asked, "Why would you say that?"

She hugged Mrs. Woods. "She picked on me every day. This time instead of me falling, she did."

Tamara had seen Mrs. Shavers running towards the elevators looking nervous. The sounds of the ambulance truck, and the ruckus from the staff and students brought back feelings of deja vu from the numerous times they were called out to her house, especially when Lasha had died. She went into the lobby and looked outside the window while everyone gathered around being noisy. The EMT's had her on the stretcher as they whisked her away. You heard Miss Williams' big mouth all the way from outside yelling. "Okay the shows over, get back to business!"

DIARY ENTRY 10

Well, I've done it again. I can't write long because I have to get ready and go see my crazy doctor. I will have me a new cell- mate when I come back in the room. I've plotted for a while now to pay her back, but I had to be very careful and plan my stuff out carefully. One thing that my mind doctor has taught me was to be very patient. And I've utilized that skill this past week. I let that bitch push me around just so I could have witnesses to verify that she in fact, did wrong things to me. Everybody in here thought that I was scared of her, and that's the way I wanted everyone to think. I had to set my pride aside for this. I have asked that bitch to join me, and she had the audacity to turn me down. For two months, I took bullshit from her. Not knocking her teeth down her throat took all the strength that I had in my body. I have been participating in Yoga classes to help me not kill her. "Channel your anger. Breathe in. Hold it in. Turn the channel to something nice and EXHALE. Relax your muscles. Let your mind take you somewhere else."

That shit works! Do you know how many times that girl has made me mentally visit some other place?

I've been to Jamaica, Hawaii, The Moon, and then I went to Saturn. If you find yourself with the same problem, you had to take yourself further than the last time that's what led me to insanity with her. She made me bleed so it was time to show her who's the Head Bitch in Charge. She tore open that envelope with me. I've kept a separate diary of everything that she did to me. I kept copies of all the written complaints that I gave to Miss Williams. My counselor knows about it: my psychiatrist knows about it, Dr. Shavers knows about it, the girls and me. A detective came out and asked me a couple of questions about the incident. I told him what I wanted him to know, and I had witnesses to back my story up. Miss Williams was nowhere to be found when it was her turn to be questioned. Some reporters were asking questions about the incident and. Miss William's assistant told the press that Mia had fallen down the stairs because of her loosened shoestrings. When Miss Williams went to the hospital to check on her niece, reporters were outside waiting for her statement about the incident. When I came back from seeing the mind doctor, Miss Williams interrupted our session to tell me to come to her office because she needed to talk to me. She explained to me what she had told the press. She lied of course, in order to save her own big behind. The last thing that she needed was bad publicity for the center. I wasn't listening to her. Everything she said went in and out until I heard those famous words.

"What do you want?"

I sat in the chair crying like I was so disturbed about what happened. "I have a copy of all the letters that I wrote about your niece bothering me." I rubbed it in as thick as possible. I grabbed a piece of paper and a pen and wrote down this.

1. *I want access to the phones at all times.*
2. *Access to the showers, anytime I want.*
3. *I want Jessica to go get my snacks at least twice a week instead of once a month.*
4. *I want visits at any and all times.*
5. *I want my male visitors to be able to go into that room on the second floor and visit privately.*
6. *I want a small television and radio in my room, but I will keep it down.*

She didn't have a problem with my demands except for number five. She told me that she couldn't do that so I told her that I was going to tell them the truth. After we debated for five minutes, she finally agreed to it. I told her to make sure that she informed her stupid security guards of my demands. I walked out of the office with a handful of passes and jumped high into the air. I almost forgot that I carried a heavy load. Ladies and gentlemen, The Oscar for best actress goes to Tamara Brown for obvious reasons.

Will you please sign my contract? Miss Williams looked at me like I was crazy, but she signed it anyway.

The first person I called using my pass was my grandma, and she told me that Diane had lost her baby last week. I didn't want to talk long and have people asking questions, but I needed to talk to her, and she was glad to hear from me. I took my shower and when I went to the room, there she was (snow white) Tina Young without her seven dwarfs. Later I found out that she was mixed. Her absent father was black and her alcoholic mother is white. I don't know what she did to get in trouble, but she looks like a good girl if I have ever seen one. She's probably one hundred pounds with wet clothes on. She's sixteen but she looks twelve. We talked for a while because she asked me a thousand questions, and I explained the rules to her. She seems okay but things aren't always the way they appear. Whenever you think your life is messed up, you come across someone else whose life is more screwed up than yours. Her mother had her prostituting when she was thirteen. She's experienced things I couldn't have imagined. I would've been locked up forever for killing everyone starting with my mother

T.B.
Two weeks later.

Welcome Back

For the two weeks that Mia was in the hospital recuperating from a fractured hip, leg, foot and a broken heart because her baby boy's heart wasn't strong enough to survive outside the womb. The girls at the center enjoyed not being annoyed by her. The atmosphere just felt clearer without her negative existence, people speculated about what really had happened that day, but she was gone, and they appreciated the peace while it lasted. Even the instructors recognized the difference in the air, but she was their boss' niece. What could they do or say? The silent celebration was over because Miss Williams was on her way to the hospital to bring her back.

Rumor spread rapidly that Mia was due to return to the center today around two o' clock. Tamara had played sick from school because she wanted to be able to lounge around and wait on Mia.

She paced the lobby's floor eating Twinkies and chips.

"It's two twenty. Where are they?" She flopped down on the sofa. **We need another damn sofa.** Tamara thought she heard a car door slam. She attempted to get off the sofa but fell back down.

"Not them," she said disappointed, looking out of the window with her elbows propped on the landing as she rested her hands on her cheeks.

Tamara had schemed with Tracey and Randie at exactly three thirty to find Yasmine (Mia's roommate) and go to the game room. Yasmine loved playing pool but she could never get anyone to play with her because she was too damn good. She always won their candy money. Money was hard to come by in here, and they wasn't going to give it all to her. Tamara had given them money to play against Yasmine. Money that she knew she would never see again. They were going to lose, but she needed her away from the room and that was worth every penny. Tamara followed

Yasmine after every class without being obvious to anyone. Yasmine was always the last one to take a shower after gym class. She went into the gym's locker room to shower before her next class started and Tamara snuck in behind her. The guard who sat at the desk was busy doing a crossword puzzle, not looking up at the students. Tamara waited between the lockers until she heard water running and Yasmine humming, The Deele's (Two Occasions.) She crept into her locker and retrieved some things from her pants pocket. "I need this." She walked out the locker room and handed something to Randie and Tracey who stood by the door in the hallway just as she had instructed them to do.

A rushing Yasmine was late again for her math class. This was the third tardy in three weeks; Ms. Jacobs was going to give her extra homework. Randie and Tracey asked her if she wanted to play pool with them at three today. "You got money?" She asked, still walking towards her class.

"Do we have money?" They laughed. "Just meet us in the game room at three. Better yet we'll come to your math class to get you," said a trash talking Tracey.

"Oh wait, Mia is coming back today," she remembered.

Randie asked with a toothpick hanging from her lips, "How much money is she going to give you since you claim you are going to take our money? All I need is an hour to get your money," she said laughing.

"We will see."

They whispered to each other as they headed back to their class laughing.

The guard looked up yelling. "Get back to class! And stop horsing around!

Randie rolled her eyes, and flipped her "the bird" as she walked on to class. "What does it look like we are doing?"

Yasmine opened the door to the classroom, causing everyone to suddenly stop what they were doing. Everyone stopped writing and stared directly at her. Kim laughed and shook her head because she had told her to stop being ashamed of that scar across her stomach (from her C-section) and take a shower with everyone else.

"Miss Davison, how many times are you going to step into my class late," the teacher asked with her glasses sitting on the bridge of her nose.

"I'm sorry."

"Write 200 times that I'm sorry for always being late to Math class, and I will learn how to be on time," she said.

Shit! "Are you serious?"

She looked serious.

"Okay."

The girls laughed.

"Ladies," she yelled.

Mia swiped her keycard to get into her room. The green dots lit up, and she turned the knob and swung in on her crutches. "Yasmine," she called out.

She used her good foot to close the door behind her. She tossed her purse and the keycard onto the dresser. She attempted to lock the door but was greeted by Tamara standing there with an open pocketknife. It startled her terribly.

Tamara laughed. "You're more messed up than I thought."

"Oh my God," she mumbled.

"Hi," she said smiling like she was actually glad to see her. "Don't call on him now missy. Were you thinking about him when you were fucking with me?" she asked, as she playfully jabbed at her with the knife. She lightly kicked her right crutch causing her to lose her balance. Tamara shook her head. "What? You didn't miss me?"

Her eyes had widened by the second. You smelled the fear on her.

"If you dare try to open up your mouth and scream, I will stick this knife right here in your main artery," she whispered.

She assured her that she didn't mention to anyone what had happened.

Tamara locked and placed the chain on the door. "We need to have a one on one before anyone disturbs us. I'm not worried about that because it's my word against yours and what I found out lady is that you are not too well-liked by your peers."

"Please don't hurt me Tamara," mumbled Mia. She snatched her crutches completely from her making her stagger to the floor. "Get on the bed," she grabbed her by the arm and tossed her onto the bed like a doll. She yelled out because she fell directly onto her fractured hip.

"Why are you doing this to me?" she asked with tears in her eyes. Her body had lain twisted on the bed. "Turn around," she said with the knife pressed into her chin. "You're not so big and bad now are you, Miss Burns? I would tell you welcome home, but I wouldn't mean it. And I don't say things that I don't mean. I have this sick, twisted honesty shit going on.

Nevertheless, I can tell you why I'm here. I wanted to tell you in person, woman to woman that I don't like you very much."

"Yeah, I figured that."

"Look at what you've done to my arms M.B. It looks like a tiger had gotten a hold of them. No one hurts me and gets away with it. You've done your share of shit to me. I took shit from you because I had bigger plans rather than whipping your ass. Oh you deserved so much more than an ass whipping M.B."

"I just was fooling around with you," explained Mia. "I play around with everyone like that."

"Well, just in case if you haven't noticed I don't play or like games and I'm not a child so I leave that to the kids. Have you talked to your fat ass auntie? Did she tell you what she wanted us to say about what happened?"

"Yeah, she told me."

"Good, just in case you wanted to change your story or confess to your BFF. My version is that you tried to push me down the stairs, and you fell instead- that's my story and I'm sticking to it. Everyone knows that you always picked on me baby," she kissed her on the cheek. She closed the knife and walked towards the door without looking back. She stopped. "If you mumble my name, or even look at me funny. I will be back. You won't know when I'm coming, where I'm at, or what I'm going to do when I find you. I got a feeling that we are going to be ace boons after all. So until next time, keep your mouth shut, sweetie. Oh, and do you need these?" She tossed her crutches in the middle of the floor and went out of the room giggling.

Mia painfully sat up on the bed in a state of shock. She was dazed as she looked in the direction where Tamara had just disappeared like she was Houdini the magician. Her body had begun to tremble uncontrollably like an addict in detox.

"She could've killed me. I need to tell someone."

She pictured Tamara's face saying. "I'll come back." She realized that she hadn't locked the door since Tamara walked out. She painfully jumped off of the bed, grabbed her crutches and locked it. She wanted to take a shower, **but she pictured Tamara hiding in the shower with a gun.** "I'd better keep this to myself. Where's Yasmine when I need her?"

It's A Full Moon

October 30, 1993
Jueves (Thursday Night)
10:47 p.m.

Tamara lay on her pregnant side, in bed watching television looking as though the *Pillow Monster* had swallowed her alive. She had a pillow underneath her head, stomach, neck and feet. She also had two pillows between her legs. She tried to sleep but was very uncomfortable because the baby was pressing against her bladder and wasn't just moving (she was dancing in there.) A thin white sheet barely covered her semi-naked body. It was burning up in the room.

Tamara glanced over enviously at Tina because she slept cozy like a baby with a smile on her face. Whoever was responsible for controlling the heat in the building must've been anemic, Tamara figured. It stayed hot all winter long. Young Guns 2 played on the television set. Even with the volume low, it still disturbed her. She became irritable to sounds and lights with each passing second (the moonlight that shone through the window bothered her terribly.) She tossed and turned as she tried to ignore the fact that she couldn't breathe and was experiencing painful cramps. Tamara had this weird look upon her face.

"Tina," she said, rubbing her stomach. "Tina!"

"What," she answered, rubbing her closed eyes. She needed a minute for her vision to clear and then another minute to register where in the heck she was. "What's wrong?"

A sharp pain shot from her lower back to her abdomen like hot lightning. She exhaled, closing her eyes and taking in a couple of deep breaths. Relax, she thought to herself.

"Are you alright?"

She yelled. "Will you stop asking me that? I can't catch my breath."

"Are you in labor?"

"No, my due date is November 9." She frowned. "If I lay down, it will go away like last week." Tamara motioned towards the dresser for her cassette player.

"Here," she passed her the player and her two favorite cassette tapes.

Their communication worked telepathically this morning. Tina went into the bathroom to pour her a glass of water. Tamara was about to ask her how in the hell did she know she was thirsty, but changed her mind because the painful cramps had returned. Tina went back into the bathroom and came out with a cold towel for her. Tamara went to say thank-you, but Tina replied, "Your welcome," before she had a chance to.

For the next five hours, she painfully tossed and turned. She thought that she was dealing with those, "Braxton Hicks Contractions," again but these cramps weren't going anywhere- they had gotten more intense.

"This pain can't possibly get anymore excruciating," she mumbled. She staggered to Tina's bed and sat next to her. "Tina, get up. Tina!"

"Huh," she gazed at the ceiling. "What Mara? What?"

"Get up girl," she pinched her. "right now."

"Ow, why did you do that?"

"I think I'm in labor."

"Wow, you think? It took you hours to realize that?"

She found the strength to chuckle. "Go tell the guard to call Mrs. Shavers now," she mumbled.

Tina ran to the end of the hallway to inform the guard to call or page the doctor.

"She'll be here soon," she said. "Just relax."

"I have to use the bathroom. Will you help me? When I walk it feels like my stuff is about to fall out."

"Come on. The baby is coming. Can I be the god-mother?" She grabbed her arm as she helped her to her feet. "So you can have my little girl on the corner selling her body with you," she said laughing.

They laughed. "That's not funny. You're obviously not hurting that bad to crack jokes on me."

She helped her to the door. "Now get out. Thank you. And yes, you can, if you promise to love my baby as much as I do."

"I promise." Tina stuck out her finger and they pinky swore.

Doctor Shavers and Miss Williams burst through the already opened door like the Feds.

"Where's Tamara?" asked a sleepy looking Dr. Shaver.

"In the bathroom," replied Tina.

Tamara yelled. "Tina!"

"Yeah."

She felt a gush of water come out into the toilet. "My water broke! Call them again."

"Tamara, open up the door," said Dr. Shavers.

"I can't," she said exhausted.

"Why not," wondered Miss Williams.

"I'm in too much- Pain! Oh my God," she moaned.

Tina walked past and opened the door. "It's already open. You didn't think to turn the knob? Two highly educated women and neither one of you thought to check and see if the door was open?" She pushed Tina out of the way. "Thank you. That will be all," said Miss Williams.

Tamara was in pain, but she agreed totally with Tina and that made her laugh.

"Can you get up?" asked Dr. Shavers.

"In a minute doctor, do the both of you have to be in here with me?"

"I called your mother and she's on her way here," Miss Williams said.

"Why did you call her? I don't want her anywhere near me or my baby."

"Your mother has to be present with you when you give birth, if it's possible. It's a state-mandated policy," said Dr. Shavers.

She wondered and asked, "Why? I am going home after I have my baby, right?"

"You have to talk that over with your mother when she gets here," Miss Williams interrupted.

"What hospital are you taking me to?"

"You are going to deliver here. We're equipped with the facilities to deliver your baby."

She tightened her stomach muscles trying to stop the contractions from coming. "What if something goes wrong?"

"We called the anesthesiologist, and she'll be here soon. The hospital is on standby. People deliver at home all the time. Don't worry, you'll be all right," Miss Williams explained as she rubbed her back in a circular motion. She jerked away from Miss Williams. "Don't do that."

They helped her to the wheelchair and pushed her to the room. Tamara asked if she could sit in the Jacuzzi and relax. "Maybe that will help you," suggested Miss Williams.

The room was average sized. It was painted light green with a relaxing wall mural of palm trees with an ocean in the background. It had the look and feel of an actual hospital maternity ward, but ten times better. Dr. Shavers reached for Tamara's hand. "Are you ready to get into the Jacuzzi?"

She paused because she had another contraction. "Yes."

"How many minutes apart are your contractions?"

"You're the doctor so you tell me," she sarcastically said as she had put on her silk gown.

"It's amazing how many girls who, in the midst of labor, are still concerned about their appearance," she chuckled. "Are you sure you want to mess this beautiful gown up?" asked the doctor.

"Yes, one of my boyfriends' bought me this gown to deliver the baby in."

The doctor chuckled. "How many boyfriends do you have?"

"Three."

"Who's the father?"

"All of them," she laughed, before another contraction ripped through her uterus. They laughed. "You can only have one father."

She brushed her hair into a ponytail. "Well, my baby is lucky. She has three daddies. Do you mind?"

She turned around. "That can be a dangerous situation," Dr. Shavers explained to her. "I can provide a DNA test for the three men to find out for sure."

"When I see her, I'll know."

Dr. Shavers checked the heart monitor and jotted down some information on her chart. "You can't always go by that."

"I'm ready to get into the Jacuzzi now. I don't really want to talk about them."

The Jacuzzi sat in the middle of Tamara's birthing room. She thought happy thoughts as the water pulsated over her body. She felt relaxed and at ease. "This is what I'm talking about," she said. Suddenly, a different feeling overcame her. "I want to get out of this thing," she said sickly as she covered her mouth. "Oh no," **I haven't sat in a tub in months, and as soon as I get the chance, I get sick**, as she filled the tub with her dinner.

"Well, that's not going to work, I see Tamara."

"I guess not, Miss Williams." Tamara rubbed her huge belly, took a deep breath, and counted to thirty as she put her nightgown back on.

"You're doing good Tamara."

"How much longer do I have until it's over?"

Dr. Shavers laughed. "There's no set time to deliver a baby. Some people experience labor for seven hours, some for twenty hours and some for forty- seven hours. It all depends on the baby and how well the mother pushes. Are you ready for your pain medication?"

"Not yet."

Dr. Shavers grabbed a pair of latex gloves from the box on the counter. "I need to examine you and see how many centimeters you've dilated."

She held her head up and rolled her eyes. "Oh, I'm tired of this checkup stuff already."

The doctor showed her the belt that she needed to put around her stomach.

"Can it wait until I'm finished having this contraction please? Damn!" Her face was frowned. "That's tight. What's that sound?"

"That's the baby's heartbeat," replied Miss Williams.

"You can hear the baby's heartbeat and her movements."

"Oh," she exhaled.

"You have dilated four centimeters. We will give you an epidural for pain."

"I wanted to have the baby naturally."

"Why have the baby naturally when you can have pain medication and be comfortable?" asked Miss Williams.

"No disrespect, but why are you in here again?"

"I'm responsible for you until your mother gets here."

"I've told you that I don't want her in here, so whatever she needs to sign let her sign them and leave."

Dr. Shavers and Miss Williams looked at each other.

Ten hours later.

The medicine had helped Tamara sleep like a baby for hours. Every hour on the hour, the doctor checked to see if she had dilated anymore, and to check her vital signs. "She's doing well," the doctor informed Miss Williams.

She sat up in the bed with tubes running everywhere possible. "I need more medicine because this is starting to wear off!" Tamara roared out. She glanced over her shoulder and… Lord behold….

"Hi Tamara," Jeanette said smiling.

"Where's Dr. Shavers," she asked Jeanette.

Jeanette placed the magazine in her lap. "You're not going to speak to me?"

"Hey," she said nonchalantly. She lay back down, turning her head and body away from Jeanette.

Jeanette said smiling, "Two more girls went into labor. It must be a full moon?"

She said with her eyes closed, "Must be because you are out. Where's my grandma?"

"I didn't have time to go and get her."

"When are we going home with grandma?"

She tried to push Tamara's hair back from her face, but she quickly turned away.

"Don't touch me Jeanette."

"Tamara, this is not the time to be angry with me. I didn't get you pregnant. I'm trying to be here for you."

"You have to be here because you're the guardian."

"I'm your mother no matter how you feel about me."

"Giving birth to a child doesn't make you a mother," she mumbled. She noticed a blue jay sitting outside her window's ledge. **If I could have my baby and fly away from here**, she wished. **I wouldn't come back.**

"Where's the doctor or the nurse with my medicine?"

She walked in on cue. "Here I am," said Dr. Shavers. "Your contractions are three minutes apart and the last time I checked, you've dilated to eight centimeters. It'll be over soon."

She had injected two types of medicine with a needle into her IV.

Tamara asked, "Why are you using two this time?"

"You need more medicine to help you cope with the pain because it will become more intense as you dilate. Try to relax as much as you can," she patted her leg. "You're doing terrific."

"I don't feel terrific."

Dr. Shavers requested that Jeanette join her in the hallway to have a serious discussion. They walked out of the room and went down the hallway, so they could talk in private. "I know that you were informed about our problem with her pregnancy."

She nodded.

"She's really ten centimeters and Miss Williams told me to give her another drug on top of the one that we were giving her to keep her comfortable and drowsy because we all know how Tamara can get. She's a feisty little thing, and she will fight with us when we take the baby away from her for tests."

"I know."

"She'll be too drowsy to know what's going on," said Miss Williams, as she joined into the conversation.

"I need to move quickly because the medicine works fast," Dr. Shavers said as she headed back into the room with Tamara.

Miss Williams handed Jeanette the documents that she needed to sign. "You need to sign the first document and have her sign the other nine documents before she's too sedated."

Miss Williams asked Jeanette, "Did you take care of everything?"

She nodded.

"Are you sure this is what you want to do?" asked Miss Williams.

"Yes, I am sure. Let's do it."

Jeanette went back in. "Tamara, can you hear me?"

She nodded "yes" slowly. "I'm so sleepy. I can't keep my eyes open. I feel so dizzy," she managed to mumble out.

"I need you to sign this paper for me Tamara. Sign your name right here. Take the pen."

Grab the pen Tamara, she told herself. **I can't do it.** Jeanette had placed the pen into her hand. "Write your name Tamara."

She said smiling, "Like I did in kindergarten?"

"Yes Tamara," said Jeanette.

"Okay. Tamara Brown," she drowsily said.

"Good girl," said Dr. Shavers. Jeanette passed each paper that she signed to the doctor, and she passed it to Miss Williams.

"Okay Tamara. Thank you. Now it's time to push."

"I'm too tired doctor. I can't push"

Jeanette grabbed her hand. "You can do it. Push hard Tamara!"

They tried to cheer her on how to push the baby out. They waited thirty minutes for her to push again, but she didn't. She was too drowsy to give birth. The baby's heart rate was dropping so they rushed her to the hospital. They had no choice but to perform a C-Section because time was running out. She felt a light pulling sensation on what she thought should've been her stomach. She faintly heard them talking to each other in the room as they operated on her. She heard a lot of crying from her little precious girl in the distance. "My baby," she said in a whisper.

"Six pounds and six ounces," someone said.

"She's six pounds even. Eighteen inches tall," someone else said.

She has a strong set of lungs on her. My goodness, Tamara thought.

"Roll her to her room," was the last thing she had heard before she woke back up three hours later. She opened up her eyes. "Where am I at?" she mumbled. She touched her almost flattened stomach. "Where's my baby?" **I thought that I was dreaming.**

Jeanette was reclined in the lazy boy chair next to the bed asleep wrapped up comfortably in a blue blanket snoring.

"Jeanette, wake up! Where's my baby?"

Tamara startled her by the way she yelled her name. "What?" She jumped up, knocking the book that sat in her lap onto the floor.

"Where's my baby? I want to see her now."

Jeanette threw the cover off of her and walked towards Tamara. "I need to tell you something."

"I want to see my baby," she said as she repeatedly pressed the help button for the doctor to come into her room.

Dr. Shavers and Miss Williams stormed into the room because they heard her all the way down the hallway. "Did you tell her?" asked Dr. Shavers directing her question to Jeanette.

Jeanette shook her head no.

"Did she tell me what?"

"I first need you to calm down so I can I tell you what happened."

She sat up. "Stop beating around the bush doctor and tell me what's going on!"

"Your baby is gone." That played in her head over and over like a broke record. "Your baby is gone," explained Dr. Shavers.

She lay back on the bed as she tried to hold back her tears. **I guess I had this coming. All the shit that I've done,** she thought.

"Gone where? What happened to her? How did she die?"

"She didn't die Tamara. You told us when you were in labor that you were willing to give the baby up for adoption until you finished school."

She was relieved. "She's not dead?" But that quickly changed to anger.

"No, but you temporarily signed your rights away." Miss Williams showed her the papers. "You and your mother both thought that it would be the best for you." She didn't say a word to Jeanette but her eyes spoke volumes. "Okay, she's not dead," she repeated. She was confused beacsue she didn't recall saying a thing like that to anyone. "I don't remember that. How can she decide anything for me? She wasn't her mother and she's not my mother."

"Look, you signed the documents," she showed her the paperwork.

She looked at that scrambled signature on each document. She sort of remembered signing the papers, but she doesn't remember discussing adoption. She tossed the papers into Jeanette's face.

"Go and get my baby! Right now!" she demanded.

"Tamara, the baby is gone with her new foster parents," explained Jeanette.

She quickly snatched the I.V. out of her arm. "Why is this shit still in my arm," blood went everywhere.

"Be still Tamara. Let me see your arm."

When she pulled away from the doctor, she'd struck her in the nose with her fist. "Don't touch me Dr. Shavers! All of you are going to hell!" Dr. Shavers held her head back and tried to stop the flow of blood. She quickly grabbed some tissue from the bathroom.

"You're bleeding all over everywhere. Bring me some band-aids for her," said Jeanette.

"I don't care! I don't care! I'm calling the police. Y'all gave my baby away! She managed to build up enough strength to get up, and she pushed Jeanette to the side.

"Tamara, you can get her back after you finish school and get your life together, lie back down."

"Fuck you bitch! Just because you didn't love me and gave me up doesn't mean that's what I wanted to do with my baby. I knew you were up to no good. You are behind all this bullshit!"

"Tamara, I just didn't want you to end up like me," she said with tears in her eyes.

"You can dry those fake ass tears up. The "Concerned Mother Show" has been cancelled. You can fool them, but that's your way to pay me back! All of you are going to pay, if I can't get her back when I'm done with school. I promise you that!"

Jeanette whispered in her ear. "You can't prove that I did this purposely," she smiled. "I'm in control."

They stared at each other without saying a word.

Miss Williams told Dr. Woods, "She needs another IV in her other arm." The doctor came in with a syringe filled with another dose of medicine to calm her down.

"You're not touching me ever again," she pointed to Dr. Shavers.

"Tamara, I'll help you. Calm down baby," explained Dr. Woods, as she quickly stuck her with the needle.

"Who has my baby," she mumbled.

"I'm not telling you until you finish school. I've talked to the family, and she seems like a good mother, and the husband is nice too," said Jeanette.

"How would you know a good mother? My baby could be with a lunatic."

The last thing she muttered out before the medicine won the battle. "Let something happen to my baby before I get to her- you will be sorry." Everyone stood there with a perplexed look on their faces. **These people are going to pay for this stunt. I'm so mad I can explode. Visit a better place and stay there for a while. Patience is a virtue. I have bigger fish to fry. I have to be able to give her the best. They all better hope that she's well taken care of, or I'm going to kill them all one by one.**

"I promise, I will come and get you, Latea` Brown."

The Beginning Of Life

On July 29, 1994, it was time for the seniors' graduation ceremony for the girls who successfully completed their classes and certificate programs. Tamara brought her grades from a two point three to a four point zero and became valedictorian of her class. She had done a complete three hundred and sixty degree turnaround from the way she once was. Her daughter was her new inspiration to try harder in school, so she would be able to provide a better life for her.

Mia and Tamara were on speaking terms (not buddies, but speaking.) Tamara had asked her to forgive her and quite naturally wouldn't you have said "Yes" even if you didn't mean it? She didn't know if she was serious, or if it was a trick, but she accepted, apologizing for her behavior and after that they had no problems. Mia had changed the way that she treated everyone else from that day on because she didn't want to live in fear of what they might've done to her. She wasn't going through that again. She learned the lesson of treating people the way she wanted to be treated.

Tina held her pencil and pretended that it was a microphone. "Tamara is going to be eighteen years old tomorrow. This is the beginning of life for this young woman. How do you feel?"

"I feel excited and anxious to meet my baby." She asked. "What time is it?"

"Noon," she said. "So today's the big day?"

Tamara lay in her bed fully clothed for the ceremony while she polished her toenails black. "I hate graduations, but I'm looking forward to tomorrow."

"I'm going to miss you lady," explained a saddened Tina.

"Me too, but those three weeks will go by before you can blink twice."

"I hope so."

"You have to be about your business because you know she wants all of us to fail. That's more money for her fat ass if we come back here. Remember, we will keep in contact by letters only because I think the phones are tapped."

"Are you coming to the graduation?"

"I don't have a ticket," Tina said. "So why are you teasing?"

"Check underneath your mattress T," Tamara smiled. She checked underneath the mattress at one end. "You play too much," she didn't find anything there and proceeded to look underneath the other end. "When did you slip this ticket underneath my mattress with your sneaky ass?"

She said grinning, "You were awake when I did it T," she laughed. "I wanted to see if I still had it."

"You do- because I had no clue you had placed this underneath here. What time is the ceremony?"

"Four o' clock. That's enough time for you to get ready white girl?"

She tossed her pillow at her. "When are we going to see my god daughter?"

"I forgot to tell you that Jeanette wrote me to tell me that the foster parents can't make it, but they will bring her to me tomorrow when I get out of here," she explained to Tina.

"So how can you sit there and be so calm about this Mara?"

She blew and waved her hands to dry them. "I have a plan mama. Don't worry."

"Am I involved in this plan?"

She shook her head.

"Why in the hell not," she questioned.

"Because if you get caught that would automatically give you more time. We need you out there, not locked up in here."

"What are you going to do? And how will this help you get Tia? You, without a scheme, are like businessmen without plans."

"I'll tell you."

They figured it was safer to discuss their plan in the bathroom from prying ears. Tamara explained that anyone could have been outside their door listening in on their conversation. Yes she was paranoid.

"You're going to do what? Have you lost your mind?"

"Shut up and listen to me," she covered up Tina's mouth. "It's going to work. It has to work T, or those people could run off with my baby."

"Have you ever thought that maybe your mother may not be telling the truth?"

She interrupted sarcastically. "You mean Jeanette?"

"Okay, Jeanette is lying and that family had already left town with her, and she's just stalling, what if she has no intention of the two of you ever reuniting again."

She applied her black lipstick onto her lips in the mirror. "That's why I have to do this today."

"Today," she probed.

"You don't put off for tomorrow what you can do today because tomorrow isn't guaranteed." replied a laughing Tamara. "I think that's the way the saying goes. My grandfather always told me that."

"It makes sense to me. What if you get into trouble for doing this Tamara?"

"You are my best-bud and I love you for being concerned about me, but I will die for what's mine- she's all I got in this world."

"Okay, Whitney Houston."

They exploded with laughter.

"I was made to believe that I was sent to this place to better my life. The real reason was because I refused to kill my baby. That's why I am here. I have the second highest grade point average in this entire center, so I kept my part of the deal, but she's not holding her end up. All I want is my baby, and I'll go on with my life without her."

"Your plan is crazy. Do you know that?"

"Maybe so, I've learned how to be crazy from the best."

Thirty minutes later.

Randie pulled down her "D" baseball cap in order to conceal her face and walked towards the stairs going west as Tracey headed east. Tamara pushed the elevator button going up, as she looked around. She wasn't supposed to be using the elevators since she wasn't pregnant, and it's been longer than six weeks since Tia was born, but she had special privileges.

Miss Williams didn't need or want a repeat of a stairwell incident, so she was granted permission to use them. She stretched her perks out as far as they possibly could go. Miss Williams didn't want Tamara to call the news reporters and tell them what her niece had done, and she definitely didn't want her to explain the circumstances behind what she allowed to happen to her baby. That extra money wasn't worth the trouble, but it looked good when it was added up for the year on paper. The girls wondered why Tamara could do whatever the hell she wanted, and that's why Miss Williams, being her first cousin, was created. No one asked questions after that.

"Oh she's family too," they rumored. "That's why."

The eleventh and twelfth grade classes were cancelled today for the ceremony, and they started assembling in the auditorium. The sounds of music came from the choir room as the ninth grade girls rehearsed the songs that were to be played during the program. The tenth graders were on a field trip today. Miss Williams didn't want to be embarrassed because it seemed as though they tended to act a fool ***every*** time they were ***expected not to***, so she sent them to Greenfield Village.

The proud family members began gathering in the gym for the ceremony. Why do parents always rush to be the first one to get good seats, but when they arrive, they discover that they weren't the only ones thinking ahead? You still end up with the seats you would've gotten if you left at your regular time.

At exactly 3:02 p.m. the sound of an alarm rocked Loving Center. A voice over the P.A bellowed, "Please form a single line, and find the nearest exit location and meet up in the front of the building!"

"What in the hell," Miss Williams wondered from the office. "These girls are going to be the death of me."

Everyone, including the teachers, quickly (and quite orderly) formed lines and walked out of the center with their ears covered up.

In the science room, smoke escaped from underneath the door. Four security guards ran into the smoke filled room with fire extinguishers and began spraying the fire that was set to three garbage cans.

"No pushing! Walk out of the center ladies and gentlemen! We have guests, show them that you know how to act," yelled Miss Williams as she turned off the alarm. She called the fire department before they had arrived and explained that the fire had been contained quickly and safely.

"Who would do something like this?" asked the guard.

"I don't know, but I'm going to have someone's head for this. They could've burned my center down," said an angered Miss Williams. "These girls are so stupid! I try and help them, but this is how I get repaid? Tell them to come back in. I have an announcement to make."

"Yes ma'am," said one of the guards.

Miss Williams pressed the talk button on the P.A. system that sat on top of a table directly behind her leather chair. "Ladies, I'm very shocked and disappointed that someone would deliberately set the garbage cans on fire in the science room or anywhere, for that matter, in this center. We have parents and friends in the building about to celebrate the girls who have completed the program and this happens. I've worked too hard to let anyone destroy my center so when and if I find out who pulled a stunt like this, they will be dealt with accordingly. Anyone with information about the person or persons responsible for this should come to my office and you will remain anonymous. Let's try and enjoy the rest of our beautiful day."

With a quick push of her feet, she swirled the office chair back around with her immediate thoughts focused on finishing the day's paperwork before the ceremony. She was surprised and actually shocked as shit to see Tamara Brown sitting in the black comfy chair that she had reserved for one-on-one talks with students and parents. It was as if she just appeared out of thin air. That wasn't the worst of it, though. Tamara held what appeared to be some kind of semi-automatic pistol. She knew this because she had seen "The Revolvers." Oh yes- she had seen them. When she was younger, her dad sometimes came home after a night of heavy drinking and would wake her. He would have his .snub-nosed .38 which he called "little Bertha" and would take her out onto the back porch, and commence to fire all six shots. Sherita would cringe and cover her ears as "little Bertha" roared only a few feet away from her.

She remembered thinking how much she would never drink or would like to be on the receiving end of those shots and now here she was staring at a mentally unstable student with a weapon that fired at least double the amount of rounds that "little Bertha" fired without re-loading.

Oh my god, Miss Williams thought to herself.

She raised her hands up. "Tamara, wait a minute. What's going on sweetie? Put the gun down," she pleaded with her.

She cocked the gun. "I'm not your sweetie Miss Williams, and I'm not going to put the gun away until you tell me what I want to know or I'll kill you right here, right now."

Sherita quickly glanced up at the door and thought. **Shit! It's locked. Damn it. There's nowhere to run.**

She held the gun with both hands pointing it directly at her head. "Don't be fucking stupid Sherita."

"Calm down Tamara. We can talk about whatever is bothering you."

Tamara thought back on one of her sessions with her psychiatrist Dr. Waters as she told her the exact same stupid thing. They could talk about whatever was bothering her. That pissed her off then and it's totally pissing her off now because neither one of them gave a damn about what was wrong with her, that was part of the program.

"You can cut the shit because I know you don't give a damn about me. Save that for a silly ass student who believes you," she carelessly waved the gun as she talked to her.

"Tamara, what's the matter?" she asked nervously.

Tamara laughed, sounding like a psychopath. She stood up from the chair, all the while keeping her eyes on the prize until she had gotten on the side of her.

"What are you about to do?" **She's going to kill you**, Sherita thought.

"I have a loaded gun with two clips in my pocket and some rope. What the fuck do you think I'm about to do with it?"

Conscience 1 thought: hit this big bitch with the end of the gun in her lying ass mouth. She's practically responsible for your baby not being here. Do something to her and let her know who she's dealing with, Tamara.

Conscience 2 thought; don't hit her Tamara. You can scare her, but don't touch her. Hit her fat ass in the stomach and see if jelly comes out. ***Do you want to go to prison? No you don't.*** Let her answer for herself, she can think on her own. I say shoot her ass. ***You would tell her that. You're such a devil.*** Goodie-Too-Shoes. She's so fat, she wouldn't feel it, but I bet you she'll think twice before she does this to another girl. Teach her a lesson Tamara. ***If you shoot this woman you will never see your baby again and the only place you will see would be a jailhouse.*** You're such a push over Angel. ***You better breathe in and out. Be cool. Get the information from her, but don't hurt anyone. I'm telling you. You better listen to me this time girl. Think about Tia.*** I ought to knock you upside the head. Why would you bring that up? ***Why wouldn't I?*** You're sneaky just like me, but I'm the bad one? ***Yes you are. Listen to me Tamara. Ow! Don't poke me with that fork,"*** said Tamara's conscience.

She tied Miss Williams' hands behind the chair while explaining that she didn't intend on hurting her, but she would if she made her. "Do you know how many girls you've pissed off simply because you owned this place? You've constantly cursed out the students and have managed to make your workers feel like shit so it could've been anyone of them that decided to kill you. "Poor Miss Williams, it's a shame that she jumped out of the window and committed suicide."

No matter how she tried not to show fear, tears strolled down her fat cheeks as she knew that Tamara was going to hurt her somehow. Tamara checked her watch. It read three thirty. "It's almost time for graduation. If you're going to make it alive, is strictly up to you, Sherita. Don't cry though. It'll work out," she used the knife from her left hand and wiped the tears from her right cheek. She used the barrel of the gun in her right hand and wiped her tears from her left cheek. "Do you remember when you told me that everything was going to be alright?"

She nodded.

"Now where's my baby?"

"I don't know Tamara," she said sobbing.

She forcefully placed the gun into Sherita's mouth. "Stop all that crying shit right now. You weren't crying when you gave my baby up for adoption," she informed her. "Now I'm going to ask you one more fucking time or I'm going to put the silencer on this gun and blow your damn brains out of your fat head."

"I swear to you. I don't know," she wailed.

"Okay one, two…"

"Get my keys off the desk and unlock that door right there," she nodded at the door. "And then you have to open up the safe deposit box and get your file out."

"I'm glad that you decided to see it my way because I really don't want to kill you Sherita."

Sweat ran from her forehead into her eyes, this caused her vision to be blurred. Tamara fumbled with the keys trying to find the right one to open up the first door. "Don't try anything funny."

She insured her that she wasn't going to.

"What's the code?"

"Six, five, four, four," she whispered.

"Six, five, four, four, six, five, four, four," it clicked open.

She quickly flipped through the charts. "Aaron, Adams, Allen, Brown. Here I go, Tamara L. Brown. Now for the truth," she sat in the chair looking through her folder. "I have the file and now I need for you to run everything down for me."

"What do you want to know?"

"Start from the beginning."

"Okay, your mother called and told me that she had a teenager who was pregnant and out of control. She'd heard from a friend about the center, and she wanted you to take advantage of the program. She said that she asked you to get an abortion, but you refused. She also thought that you were pregnant by a married man."

"What?" she laughed.

"That's what she told me? She visited me a week before you two- you and your grandmother came up here and paid for a month in advance. She told me that you had been beating on her, and she wanted you out of her house. She knew that babies were not allowed on the premises, but I'm going to change that soon. You could've stayed here, had the baby and went home with her permission or sent the baby with foster parents and would've gotten custody once you'd completed the program. She told me to call her when I received any news about your pregnancy or when you went into labor. She paid me extra not to let you know about any of this." She coughed. "When you went into labor she told me to give you something to make you incoherent but make sure it was something safe enough for you and the baby and. I did. She had me to believe that you called her and threatened to kill yourself and the baby if you couldn't leave with her after the baby was born, but she was too afraid of you coming back home with her. She gave you the papers to sign after the medicine had started to take effect. That covered me from being liable and that protected her as well. We kept you sedated for three days until she took Tia home to her foster parents."

"Who are her foster parents?"

"Take a look at the file Tamara because there's more that you need to know."

"What?"

"Look in the folder."

Tamara opened up the vanilla folder and began reading the documents. "I don't remember discussing anything about an adoption. She came across two certificates of birth documents in the folder. "Wait a minute," she whispered to herself. She looked at Miss Williams with her mouth wide open. "Is this information on here correct?"

"Yes it is."

"I have twi-"

"Yes, you have twins Tamara."

"A little boy and a girl, she named them Caylyn and Jaylyn Brown. They are fraternal twins but they look like you."

She quickly searched for the name and the address of the family that had her babies. She dropped the folder out of disbelief. "I can't believe this. I've talked to them and have seen some of them and not one of them told me."

Tamara rested her head on the back of the chair.

"She had us all fooled. When you had your ultrasound, we discovered that you were carrying twins and she said she was going to take care of everything."

"Mind if I take this?" She stuck the folder into her shirt. "I'm about to untie you but you still better act right. Okay?"

She quickly shook her head quickly. "Okay."

"Thank you for the information and thank you for the proof," she shook the tape recorder that she had used to record their conversation since she came out of the closet. She played some of it back to let her know that she wasn't bluffing.

"The way I see it, I've talked to an attorney and everyone's going to be in a shit load of trouble if I don't get my babies back. Let's see, you accepted a bribe from an ex-mental patient, I was drugged and tricked into signing consent papers to give my babies away. You-"

The phone rang. "Can I get it?"

She slouched down, untying her. "Get it."

"I'll be down in a minute." She kept her eyes on Tamara. "Okay, start the ceremony." She yelled. "I said, I'll be there in a minute," she hung up.

"Jeanette gave up all her rights as a parent to my grandmother, and she didn't approve of me being here. Jeanette lied to you about everything. I wasn't even living with her; I was living with my grandmother. I have never beat on Jeanette, in fact, it was the other way around, and she wanted to fight me all the time. Jeanette lost her baby and she hated me afterwards and this was her way of paying me back because I moved back at home with my grandmother. Jeanette is a mental case who hates her own child."

"What took you so long to tell me?"

"Would you had believed me if I told you?"

Miss Williams paused for a moment.

Tamara answered for her. "No, you wouldn't have because money motivated you. You are just as guilty as she was, so either of you can place blame. You two were in on it together. You can't tell on her without prosecuting yourself. I'll make a deal with you. If you don't mention this ordeal and as long as I get my babies back, we are straight. I won't mention this scam to anyone, but I will have to let Jeanette know so I can get them back without any hassles. You know, I still have that reporter's name and number. She'll love to hear this story. You scratch my back and I'll scratch yours. See you at graduation," she placed her weapon into her pocket and walked out. Miss Williams' body collapsed onto her desk as it hit her how close she had just stared death in the face. "How am I supposed to go downstairs and pretend like nothing happened?" She started to weep heavily and then she laughed hysterically. She thought to herself, **I'm going to have to see a psychiatrist after today**

"When did you come up here?" asked the security guard.

"I came up here with Miss Williams after the fire. She had seen me in the hallway and asked me to come into her office with her. She congratulated me on my good grades. You didn't see us?"

"No, I saw her, but not you."

"And you call yourself a security guard? You're fired Yolanda," she laughed, but kept on stepping. "Stop watching those soap operas and do your damn job."

DIARY ENTRY 12
Reunited
August 1, 1994

The day of the graduation was very interesting, but nothing like the day I got out of that place. I know Miss Williams was glad when I left the center because she doesn't have to peep around corners any longer searching for me. Well, that's a lie because I told her to watch her back because she never knew if I would be behind the door or underneath her table. Based on what they'd done to me, they all should watch their backs from this day forward until I die.

Tina and Tracey cried like babies after the graduation. Randie and I, of course, were too hard to let anyone see us shed any tears. She's going to miss me, and I'm going to miss her as well, minus the sexual stares she gave me from time to time, but she's the true definition of a gangster bitch, and she didn't care who knew it. Shit, Randie had more girls in there, than most guys who I knew out on the streets. She's not a dumb girl; I think she likes being stuck in that place because of the girls. She'd helped me study for my biology and history tests numerous times, so she's not stupid by a long shot. I had threatened to knock her teeth down her throat because she had a problem with licking people. Yes, I said licking people. That was nasty and weird. Out the blue she would just lick you. She said that I tasted like LEMON with her crazy ass. How can someone's skin taste like a lemon? Was I sour or what? I always took showers, so I know my skin wasn't salty or sour. Randie stood five foot eight inches tall. She boyishly carried around two hundred and ten pounds. Her complexion was caramel. She kept her short hair whipped at all times because she could curl her own hair. She wasn't an ugly girl, but she carried herself like a boy. Her body, I would imagine, was shaped like a girl, but she wore baggy clothes. It was apparent that she was the guy in the relationships. I've never seen her wear a dress or any make up, not even lip-gloss. A lot of the girls thought that I was gay because I hung out with her and Tracey. At first, I talked to them because I needed them to carry out my plans, but eventually we all became close friends. If they had to think that I was gay to get the job done, then so be it, because I'm secure about my sexuality. My girl Tracey was trouble, but not quite as bad as Randie, She was the complete opposite of Randie. She was five feet four inches tall. She weighed one hundred and ten pounds. She was mixed (Hispanic and Black) with acne spots all over her face. She had long pretty hair. She knew that Randie was gay but that didn't stop their friendship. How friendly were they? Who knows? Really, who cares?

Mia and Randie didn't like each other, but they'd had an unspoken rule not to test each other's power. Mia was bigger than her, but I think Randie would've tapped that ass.

I'm concerned about little Tina since I'm gone. Females didn't like her and she never did anything to anyone. I asked Randie to protect her until she's free, and I will personally come up there and pay her fifty dollars when I pick Tina up from the center in three weeks. She'll do it because money moves mountains, especially when it's pertaining to Randie. Bad shit motivated her also, but she'll do it quicker for money. You know I had to throw in the deal for her not to have sex with her because she would have, without a doubt, made her sleep with her to protect her. She liked her, but Tina didn't care too much for her, not even as a friend. I can say that Tina was my first true friend, so I have to protect her.

Nikki was cool too, because she was the one that brought the gun and knife to the center. I don't know where it came from but I didn't have it loaded anyway. She slipped it into my pocket when she had visited me two months ago. We hugged and she dropped it into my pocket smoothly. My baby Tyrese had visited me all the time too. Charles didn't visit that much, but he sent me money quite often, that's all I wanted anyway.

My grandmother, Ashley, Lexis, Jeanette and Marion were present at the graduation. Diane had stayed at home because she wasn't feeling well, or so they claimed. I heard that Lynette is addicted to crack cocaine. She had started smoking weed to help loosen her up before a show. She then joined with the wrong dancers who introduced her to snorting cocaine before each show. The club closed down, but she was hooked like metal to a magnet. She couldn't afford to purchase the expensive stuff so she went to the cheapest drug to get her high, which was crack. She was in a rehab center because she had started to steal money from the grandma and didn't have anywhere else to turn to. She sold grandma's curling irons and her tennis bracelet that granddaddy had bought her. Grandma was furious. She would sneak around the house like a mouse looking for anything that wasn't nailed down to the floor. Nikki told me that Lynette had looked horrible. I know you're wondering about the baby. I had twins and they hid it from me. I didn't say a word to Jeanette the entire time that she was at the center. I had to think about how I wanted to plan this one out. Tyrese came the next morning to pick me up around eight o'clock on my birthday. We went to a restaurant for breakfast and went downtown and talked to the attorney Karen Less. She explained to us that what they'd done to us as parents wasn't legal. I could press charges against everyone who had participated in the situation about Tia. (I keep calling her Tia. Caylyn) I found out a lot of valuable information. Jeanette wasn't my legal guardian, so she couldn't have placed me in the center in the first place. Grandma was the one that was supposed to have done that. They had me incapacitated when I signed the bogus foster parents/adoption papers. You have to go through the court system to get custody of a child.

Jeanette had made copies of a girl who really gave her kids to foster parents' papers, but she didn't go to court to legally put my kids in foster care. Another thing was that, they didn't get consent from my kids' father to put them in foster care or up for adoption, which are two different things. By him not signing away his rights as a parent, none of this could possibly be legal if she didn't go to court. Karen called her sister who was a detective at the ninth precinct on Gratiot and explained our situation to her. She told us to meet her in her office at two o'clock. I had gotten on the phone with her and gave her names and numbers of the guilty people. She talked to Tyrese and asked him a couple of questions. We shook hands with attorney Less and headed back to the eastside. We searched high and low for answers and the address of the person who had my babies. They had relocated so I looked for Lynette. I knew she was on drugs, and I would be able to get information out of her with the offer of a few dollars. She had gotten out of the rehab four days before I had arrived home, so I know she would be up to her old tricks. Just my luck, Mr. Love was playing the lottery at the corner store. I said what's up and made small talk until I asked him if he'd seen or knew where Lynette hung out because the family was worried about her. Surprisingly, he had given me the address, the house color, the cross streets and everything. It made me wonder if he on that shit himself or just extremely fucking nosey. We followed his instructions and sure enough, we pulled up in front of the house on Crane Street, and she was walking onto the porch with a comforter set underneath her arm. Oh my god. She looked like a zombie. I couldn't believe this was my pretty auntie that stood in front of me no bigger than a second with her two front teeth missing. As I looked at her, I instantly thought back to the last time that I had seen her. It was the day that I had left and went to the center. She told me to stay strong and take advantage of everything that this place had to offer me. She also told me that she didn't agree with me going to this place, but she couldn't do anything about it. I remembered turning around and she had tears rolling down her face. I noticed at that exact moment that she really cared about me. All those arguments we had didn't mean a thing. She never hit me, no matter what I had said or had done to her.

But Alexis that was a different ball game. She would pick up the closest thing to her and try and knock the fool out of me. We fought all the time, like a cat and a dog. I had quickly wiped my eyes because they started to water. Maybe the wind had gotten into my eyes, or was it my allergies? (Smile) Anyway, I had gotten out of the car and hugged and kissed my auntie on the cheek. She smiled at me and burst into tears. I grabbed her and we cried together right on the sidewalk in front of the house looking crazy. Lynette started laughing and that had stopped the crying process. Before I could ask her any questions she said," You're looking for Diane right?"

It shocked the hell out of me. "Yes, I am."

I didn't have to bribe her with money because she sang like a canary, telling me everything and more. I had offered her some money, but she wouldn't take it from me, but when Tyrese thanked her and handed her the money, she snatched it from him and said with a smile, "I won't take the money from my niece, but I will surely take it from you. Thank you."

I told her that I would be back for her. She helped me big time, and I will come back for her. We pulled off and she waved good-bye until we turned the corner. I was mad as hell when I found out that Diane and Marion had my twins the entire time and no one informed me. It wouldn't have been so bad if they had told me that they had them. Both had good jobs, and they were family, so I wouldn't have worried so much. Did they think I wouldn't come back for my babies? I don't understand their plans but eventually I would've found out. Dark secrets always found their way to the light, my granddaddy always said. Then I found out that Diane and Marion separated last year. I guess she got tired of him whipping her ass. Diane was working out in Taylor, Michigan as a third grade teacher. Marion stopped drinking; and checked himself into an anger management program for six months. He had finished his last semester in school, and started a construction company in Bloomfield Hills, Michigan. He keeps in touch with the family for Sunday dinners and holidays. He wanted Diane back, but she claimed too much damage was done and she's not ever going back to him.

You thought he was fine before? Rehabilitated and fine as ever. Jesus Christ. No wonder why she moved to Taylor. Give a handsome man like him some money and he's unstoppable.

We met with Detective Davison at two o'clock sharp. I had shown her the documents, and I let her listen to the tape of Miss Williams' confession. She asked her about the placement of my babies. She claimed that it was just a temporary placement until I came home. She lied of course to cover her fat ass, (which was a lot of lying to cover that big ass of hers.) She gave Diane's current address and place of employment. I didn't ask anyone in the family because they couldn't be trusted. Mrs. Davison was about her business; you could see it in her eyes. She had three children of her own, so she personally understood how we felt. She talked to Jeanette and had explained the situation to her about the fact that she had kidnapped her grandchildren, and I could've pressed charges. She called and talked to grandma for a while, and that's when I found out that Jeanette had lied and said that I didn't want them. I listened closely to this conversation because she was going to ask her questions that I wanted to know for some time now. "Did you want Tamara to go to that center?"

"You didn't- so why did you agree to it?"

"I didn't want to get in the middle of that. That's her daughter."

"Didn't you have sole custody of Tamara since she was born?"

"Yes, but what could I have done? She's the mother."

"Did you two ever go to court to reestablish her parental rights?"

"No."

"Well Mrs. Brown, you were the only one that could've made the decision to place Tamara into that center. You were her mother no matter who gave birth to her. She had signed away her ability to make any important decisions about Tamara. That's irrelevant now, but we need to find Diane, so we can get Tamara's babies back."

Detective Davison had explained the sensitive subject to her some more. I got on the phone with grandma, and she told me to come to the house and get her because we were going to get my babies without the police being involved. She made copies of the paperwork and told me that if everything didn't go smooth, I was to come back and see her. She told me that she was going to call and warn Diane about my visit, and to have the babies ready and give them to us or risk going to jail for kidnapping if she didn't turn them over to me. We were filled with joy; ecstatic was more like it. After we left the office, Tyrese did eighty all the way to the house. We were right up the street, less than three minutes away from the precinct. However, it took forever to get to Diane's house. Diane called grandma on her cell phone and asked to speak to me. She told me that she was waiting on me to call her. She told Jeanette to give me her phone number and address, but she never did. She had told Diane and Marion that I had threatened to kill the babies, and that I didn't want to see them. She had planned on finding someone to adopt my babies for real but Marion said he would keep them because they were family. Plus Jeanette obviously couldn't put them up for adoption because she wasn't their parent. I had a million and one questions to ask her, and she answered every question that I had thrown at her. Diane wanted to bring the babies to the center for me to see them, but Jeanette lied and said that babies weren't allowed at the center for protective reasons. They couldn't live there but they could have visited. Diane figured that if I had seen them, I would've eventually changed my mind. She said on the weekend she was going to call around and find me because my kids were a hand full. She said with laughter, "I want you to come and get your little bambinas. I love my great niece and nephew, but they are bad as hell, like you were when you were younger. I'll have them ready on the front porch with their things when you get here. I would never kidnap anyone's child Tamara. You should know me better than that. When you had seen my name on the paper why you didn't call me first?"

"I don't know. I thought that everyone was in on the secret with Jeanette. I'll see you shortly okay."

Oh, when I first laid my eyes on my two beautiful children sitting in the middle of the floor playing with their blocks. I hugged them tightly until Caylyn said, "Move," as plain as an older girl would've said. All of us laughed.

Tyrese immediately extracted Jaylyn out of my arms and headed to the couch with him. He said, "Hey big fella," with a few tears falling down. "Eyes," Jaylyn said, as he pointed to his eyes. They looked just like their father who, at this very moment, I wasn't so sure as to who it was. He played and talked with them for hours. Diane had taken pictures every month of the twins for memories for me. We had packed as much stuff that his car could hold, but Diane will bring the rest of their toys and beds in her truck tomorrow after work. I was mad at Diane at first until I had seen how well she took care of my babies. And to know that she wasn't trying to take them from me made me feel better. They had the best of everything; shoes, clothes, toys. You name it; they had it. How am I going to compete with that? Jeanette had her fooled about the whole thing, but I, in the long run, was lucky that Diane had agreed to care for them while I was away. Jeanette didn't hurt me like she had planned to. She actually has helped me. I have a high school diploma along with a certificate as pharmacy technician, so I say to Jeanette, thank you. You opened the doors up for me, and I've learned new, valuable things. I've met my best friend in the whole wide world. Yes, I'm still a little dysfunctional, but I know when to be dysfunctional and to whom. I have one person to blame for all of my problems. It'll take a while before I can execute my plan, but it's going to be a big payoff for me. You just watch.

We're living with Tyrese until it's time for Tina to get out of the center. Next week, I'm going to search for us an apartment in Texas. I've saved two thousand dollars over the months that Tyrese and Charles had sent me money. Tyrese is going to take me to Texas to look and pay for an apartment for us while I'm in school. Every six months, he's coming to visit me and will bring the kids back home with him for two weeks, maybe. My babies are some busy bodies. They never sleep at the same time so we can't get any sleep. Tyrese found a real job to mask his drug dealing money. He never touched the drugs or was within twenty feet of it, so he would never get tangled up in it. No one would dare rat him out to the authorities because the last man who did is making dirt worm sandwiches, six feet underground. I'm going to be a little busy over the next three weeks getting ready to move to Texas, not to mention getting acquainted with the twins, so I'll write in you as soon as I can. I picked Texas for a very special reason.

Tamara

False Identity

Eight months later.
Friday, March the 13th

Tamara and Tina had adjusted well in Mansfield, Texas. Tamara went to school part time and had found a job working at Graham's Factory Warehouse as a secretary. Tina had a job working as a waitress at The Chicken Heaven restaurant full time. They'd worked opposite schedules so someone would always be home with the children. When they arrived in Texas, they had switched identities for Tamara's important scheme that she currently worked on. Tamara was dating an investigator who'd tried to help her get the information on a specific person who she was looking for. However, he couldn't find any info on the target so she stopped dating him.

Tina tried to convince Tamara not to do this crazy thing that she had planned, but her friend wouldn't listen to her. She'd never seen her as adamant about anything in her life, and she'd seen her determined before. However, this plan was different and was going to change their lives forever, she explained to her. "If you stick with me and do as I say, you we will be okay for the rest of your life."

Two pictures of a brown-eyed Tamara hung on the wall behind her desk: "Employee of the Month," for October and November. She was well liked on her job; never was late, never called off in seven months and her work performance was terrific. She'd managed to get close to her male supervisor (the owner's son) by the old- *'my car won't start routine'* four months ago. And after one week of picking Tamara (Tina Young) up, he was caught like minnows in a fisherman's net.

She took a load off in the chair staring at her fancy blue dress that hung on a hook on her closet. "Why would I wear something this fancy to the movies?"

Looking at the dress brought back memories of Diane's wedding.

She glanced at her watch and noticed that he was fifteen minutes late, and he hadn't called to tell her that he was on his way. She dialed his number and it went straight to voicemail.

"You have ten minutes to call me with those magic words: I'm on my way, or I'm staying home."

Meanwhile, Tina relaxed outside in the backyard underneath the patio's umbrella in the shade sipping on a daiquiri, as the kids played in the pool splashing the water in each other's face.

"Don't hit him Caylyn," yelled Tina. She stuck her tongue out at her; smiled, and then continued to splash the water in his face. "Didn't I say stop it, Caylyn!"

"Leave me alone," she yelled. "You not my mama," she replied.

"You better watch your mouth," Tamara yelled from the bedroom window.

Michael was at the factory upset because instead of being in his car on his way to Tina's house, he was stuck in the office firing people. "Special delivery from mother," he handed out ten pink slips to the men responsible for twelve shiploads of merchandise that were damaged because they weren't properly packed. Workers on lines five, six and nine were let go. Five and six had done the packaging, and the idiots on nine were supposed to handle the quality inspection. Mrs. Graham was too furious to fire them so she sent Michael instead. "I would kick every last one of them in the ass before I let them go so it's better if you do it."

Mrs. Graham loved Tina as a secretary, but she didn't approve of them dating because she was too young for him. He was thirty-four and she had just turned twenty-one, according to her ID (which we knew was false).

He really liked her and this was the first time in his life that he'd told his mother where to stick her opinion about a girlfriend of his. He'd fell head over heels in love with her. TY (is what he called her) was different than any other woman that he ever dated, he explained to his mother. "I think I'm going to ask her to marry me someday."

His mother didn't like the way those words sounded. Her eyes bucked, her mouth was twisted and she headed straight to the cabinet to pour a stiff drink (bourbon was her choice) with no ice. Forget the glass she drank from the bottle. "Are you nuts Tr-?"

He intercepted. "Don't call me that mother. I hate my middle name."

He felt like they had too much in common to let her escape like their love for football, basketball and wrestling plus both of them loved music with a passion.

Out of four months, they had never slept together and never kissed on the lips. She told him that she was saving it for that special one, and she thought that kissing on the lips was "out right nasty". That's what made him want her even more, but his mother had sworn that she was a tramp, until he confessed that they hadn't crossed those lines yet. She teased him saying that she really didn't want him. "I have to go mom." He said abruptly. He didn't feel comfortable talking to his mother about *THAT!*

He fired the men, left the building and ran through traffic lights and stop signs trying to make it to pick her up. He had a surprise for her this evening, instead of going to the movies she was going to a party at his mother's house. His new girlfriend had a surprise for him also. She wasn't who she says she was and he would soon find out.

He stopped at the store to purchase some liquor hoping to loosen her up before she went to the party. He wasn't an alcoholic, but he must have at least one drink in the morning to start his day off right, and at least two drinks of Scotch with two ice cubes every night before bed or sex. He would probably drink himself senseless if he knew the real identity of his TY. She told him that she lived with her best friend, and her twins. She had to watch them while she went to work and school. He offered to pay for a babysitter for the kids, so she could spend the night with him, but she refused. He asked if he could come and stay the night with her, but one look at those babies and she would have been busted. (I know it's tricky, but keep up with me people.)

Tamara wasn't attracted to him and she wouldn't be next year, or the year after that, but he had something that she wanted- Money. It was something that she felt that she deserved. She couldn't stomach spending the night with him, but she was willing to do almost whatever she had to do to build up his trust and knock down that brick wall that he unknowingly had around him; his mother.

"This here is some personal shit that I have to take care of because you and life left me no choice. You got something that I need, plus I can't think of a better person who doesn't deserve it more than you." She started singing Biz Markie's, You got what I need..." She chuckled. "You spoiled brat."

Last week, she'd cursed him out because he had stopped by the house without calling first. Tyrese had left the house less than ten minutes before Michael had pulled up unannounced. That could have created an ugly situation.

Even though Tyrese and Tamara didn't go together, he came to town and spent the night with the children from time to time. They might not have been an item, but he paid the rent and all the utilities to keep the courts out of their business. She didn't want to mess up her good thing with either one of these men because both of them took good care of her.

Tamara's cell phone rang.

"Hello Michael."

"Hello sweet thing. Are you ready to go because I'm around the corner?"

She laughed. "I'll be the fine girl standing outside in the blue dress waiting for you when you arrive," she removed the smile off of her face as soon as they hung up.

He was a very superstitious person, so saying good-bye was one thing that he didn't say because that sounded too" final" to him. She ran to the back door and told Tina that she was about to go. "Ooh look at you," Tina said.

She stepped out on the patio and kissed the kids on the cheeks. "Bye."

Caylyn waved, and continued to splash the water almost wetting her mother. Jaylyn cried like he always did whenever she left the house without him.

Michael whipped into the driveway with the music bumping loud. Her nosey neighbors eyed her with contempt or maybe it was jealousy as the different men came in and out of her home. She didn't care what any of them thought because all her needs were being met by her male friends, so to hell with them and their biased opinions of her.

He shut the car door once she got in the car. "Will you turn that shit down a little?" He laughed, turning it down. "I thought you loved music?"

"I love music, but I have sensitive ears and besides my heart's bumping hard with the music."

"No kiss, no hug, no thank you for the dress?"

"I told you that I don't kiss in the mouth because it's germy. I don't know where your lips or your mouth has been."

He gently rubbed her leg before she knocked his hand down. "You're crazy, but that's why I love you so much," he told her.

She looked out of the window. "There are a few other reasons why you should love me, but I can't tell you right now."

"Why not," he enquired.

"I'll tell you later," she smiled.

"Give me a kiss and stop playing," he leaned over to kiss her and she gave him her cheek. "You look good tonight baby girl," he said, trying to rub her leg again saying, "Almost as good as me."

"Thank you," she slapped his hand off of her leg again. "Keep your eyes and both hands on the steering wheel.

"I see you're in your sarcastic mode tonight," he said.

"I see you're in your freaky mode."

"Can we get freaky tonight after the dinner party? I promise I won't drink tonight." **What am I going to do now? He has to drink! Okay calm down you have all night to think of something,** Tamara thought. She looked out of the window daydreaming as he did eighty all the way to his mother's house. Out of the blue she turned the radio down and asked him with a serious look on her face. "Do you have another girlfriend or children?"

"No- I'm not cheating, and no I don't have any kids."

"I better not find out that you have a child ten years down the line."

He grabbed her hand and kissed it. "I promise. I love you and only you."

He pulled into the driveway at his mother's mansion. There were at least twenty-nine cars parked on her field next to the twelve thousand square foot home. Tamara got out of the car speechless. She didn't even notice Mrs. Graham when she walked up to them. "I said, "Hello Tina."

"Oh, I'm sorry Mrs. Graham. Your house had me in a trance."

"It does that to everyone the first time," she said show-boating.

Michael interrupted. "She'll have a house like this soon."

One day, Tamara thought to herself.

She staggered to the other side of the car to kiss and hug her son. "I'm sure that's what she's working on," Mrs. Graham sarcastically mumbled.

"Mother," Michael said.

Mrs. Graham was a slim framed, petite sixty year old vibrant woman. Her hair was a salt and pepper color, and it was always in a well-kempt ponytail. Her big golden brown eyes and high cheekbone structure made her face memorable. She didn't look a day over forty with her high yellow smooth-textured skin; only thing that made her look old were the glasses that sat on the bridge of her nose.

Michael, her thirty four year old baby, stood tall, young and handsome, looking like an exact replica of his mother, but a shade darker. His hair was fine and curly and he was never seen wearing anything other than a suit that matched from his sunglasses to his shoes. Women fell for his expressive style, but what drove them crazy was the way he smelled. His cologne preceded him through the door before he had entered. His entire dresser was occupied with different, good smelling, expensive cologne.

Tamara had heard her sarcastic comment indeed, but hadn't responded to it because she was visualizing herself owning this home, or one just like it. Michael decided to walk away from the soon to get "hostile situation."

"Shall we attend the party? Follow me," he grabbed Tamara's hand. "I have some people whom I want you to meet, darling."

The party was underneath a huge white tent in the backyard. It was beautiful back there. Twenty tables were covered with green tablecloths, and eleven tables were covered with white ones. Candles were lit in the middle of each table. The chairs were green and white to match the color theme. Mrs. Graham's table had an ice sculpture of "herself" sitting in the middle with fans blowing cold air onto it to prevent it from melting. Tamara thought the ice sculpture was a tad bit unnecessary, but kept the thought inside. "*Very narcissistic." A sculpture of yourself Mrs. Graham, how self-absorbed?"*

Michael dragged Tamara around showing her off like she was a trophy that he had won. The women turned their noses up at her wishing that they were on his arm, and the men envied him wishing that she was their young lady.

The band members talked among themselves as they stood on the makeshift stage in between sets, appearing bored from the music that the old-timers requested for them to play. Tamara wished that she was at home with the family watching movies, but she had a job to do. Michael asked her to dance with him, but she told him that she was too embarrassed to dance in front of large crowds. But he forced her to the dance floor anyhow.

Two hours have passed by and this party is still boring, Tamara thought. **I have to do something before I die of boredom.** Tamara rose from the table. Everyone had their eyes glued on them the entire time. She decided that if they wanted to stare, she would have given them something to look at. "I'll be right back."

He stopped eating. "Where are you going?"

"I have a surprise for you," she switched away from him with a half grin. The men watched her as she went up to the band and whispered something to the piano player.

"What is she doing?" wondered Janet, one of Michael's cousins.

Janet popped her husband upside the head because of the way he ignored her foaming at the mouth gawking at Tamara. She had made him spill his drink on himself. The band started playing, "Let's stay together," by Al Green." Tamara grabbed the microphone. "Ladies and gentlemen, I would like to dedicate this song to Mrs. Graham and Michael. She started singing. "I'm so in love with you..."

She had the guests on their feet shaking their rear ends including Mrs. Graham. Since she was the birthday lady, Tamara took her song requests which were "What's going on," and "Human Nature." They loved her singing so much that they had her sing two more songs before she had to tell them she was done.

Michael sat smiling at the table because whenever he thought all of her talents were displayed; she threw a new thing at him making him proud that she belonged to him. "I'm ready to go home. I need to talk to you about something," Michael told her.

"You have a beautiful voice Tina."

"Thank you," she said to the strange woman.

He excused the both of them from the table. "Let's go."

Oh my goodness! All that singing, I had forgotten to get my plan together for tonight, she thought.

"Good night everyone, I'm about to go home," declared Michael.

Mrs. Graham hugged and kissed Michael, and then she turned around and gave Tamara a forced hug. "Thank you for a great time. I'll see you Monday. We'll do lunch."

"I enjoyed myself Mrs. Graham," said Tamara.

They walked back to the car. He went to hold her hand, but she pulled it away, pretending to scratch it even though it wasn't itching.

"I can't stay out all night because Tamara has to go to work tonight."

"You can't live your life babysitting her damn kids. What would you do if I asked you to marry me?"

That question shocked her. "I don't know, but we'll worry about that when and if we ever cross that bridge."

"Take me home first and I'll find a babysitter for them, and I'll come back to your house when they're squared away in bed. "

"You're going to leave them home alone?"

She laughed. "Do I look stupid to you? I'll pay the neighbor's teenage daughter, a couple of dollars to watch them until Tamara gets home."

He stared at her. "What's your problem?"

"Nothing," she replied.

"Can u you promise me that you won't leave me hanging tonight?"

"Yes."

He was disappointed that he was going to have to wait until later to see her. At least for the first time in four months she'd agreed to spend the night with him. He gave her two hundred dollars to take care of the baby-sitting fees, and for the cab fare back to his house. He kissed her on the cheek. "I'll see you baby."

"I'll see you later daddy," she got out of the car with her shoes in her hand. "I'll see you later alligator."

"After a while crocodile," he smiled as he watched her go into the house before he pulled off.

The neon clock on the wall read twelve twenty two in the morning. She busted into Tina's room and all three of them lay in the bed out like a blown fuse. She called Tina's name. She lightly shook her, and then she started shaking her harder. "Tina," she whispered.

"What do you want Tamara?"

"Get up! I need to talk to you about something very, very important."

She exhaled deep, sitting up carefully making sure she didn't wake up the kids. "What are you up to now?"

"I have a bizarre plan that involves you."

"Everything that you do is bizarre to me Mara. What do I have to do now?"

She gave her that devilish grin, that one that she flashed whenever she's about to do something outlandish. She said laughing, "I need for you to sl..."

"What!!" she yelled.

Dear Diary;

Today is Sunday, March 15, 1995. Friday was a long prosperous night. I hope you're ready for some juicy stuff because I have a lot that I need to get off of my chest starting with the night after the party. I came home and got Tamara (Tina) and I had to run the entire plan down to her so I guess now I have to break it down for you. Last month, Tina had confided in me that she wanted a child of her own someday, but she didn't see it happening because she was always too busy with my kids. I told her that she was going to get well-reimbursed for the patience and the loyalty that she'd shown so far. Getting to the point, Michael wanted me to spend the night with him; I didn't want to, but I had to. At times, I have to do things that even make me sick to the stomach. On the way home I thought of a good plan to help me- well, for us to get closer to our destiny. I know I'm rambling; be patient my dear friend. Michael wants to bear a child with me, but I wouldn't dare to go there with him. I can't have sex with someone that I have no feelings for. I could care less how much money he has, I can't bring myself to do it. I have to draw the line somewhere. I called Michael that night and asked him if he would like for me to tie him up to the bed and he said yes with such delight. Yes, tie me up baby. I will be your slave-- were his exact words. I asked him if he wanted to make me pregnant tonight and he said yes without hesitation. I'd talked to Tina and at first she wasn't with it until I explained the full benefits of her doing what I had asked. Money will make most people do some crazy stuff. What would you do for a Klondike Bar? What wouldn't you do for money? That's a better question. The girl next door Tamika, let her daughter come over to my house to watch the kids overnight. I told her that we both were scheduled to go to work tonight and we couldn't call off or we would get fired. I paid her daughter forty dollars and gave her mother forty dollars for letting her stay. I told Tamika that we had to work until eight o' clock, and if she did a good job with them today, I would pay her well to keep them if I needed her again. I called Michael and told him to leave the key underneath the doormat so I can act like I'm a burglar breaking into his house. I did that, so he wouldn't see Tina come in with me. She took a shower and got dressed and I called the cab and we headed straight to his house. Well actually, we had the cab driver drop us off at the corner just in case Michael was looking out the window for me. You always have to plan ahead. We successfully crept into the house. I was praying that he didn't see or hear us come in. I directed her to hide in this room that he barely used. It was kind of empty and it looked as though he used that room for storage. His house was so big, he could've had someone living with him, and he wouldn't even have realized it. I told her to stay hiding in the closet or somewhere in the room, just in case he came in there for something. I said, "I'll come back and get you, when I'm ready for you." I went upstairs and Michael was lying across his huge bed, penis at attention. "Michael!" I yelled out.

He removed the blindfold from his eyes and jumped up quickly. He asked me what was wrong. I turned my back away from him and requested that he put his clothes back on. Why he wondered. You're taking all the fun away from it. I wanted to be the one that takes them off of you. That was the only excuse that I could come up with. Are they back on? I asked him. He put his T –shirt and his boxer shorts back on. I pulled my handcuffs out of my purse and pushed him onto the bed and handcuffed him to the bed. I had placed his blindfold back over his face with another silk scarf of mines over it tightly so it wouldn't move out of place. I tied his big ugly feet to the bed- posts. I would never let anyone tie my ass up to anything. I went downstairs and poured him a drink and laced it with two strong sleeping pills. I went into the room and got Tina, and we went upstairs. Before we went upstairs, I explained to her again what to do. We gave the medicine time to work, plus he had been drinking. As they were having sex I had to stay in the room talking into his ear, so he wouldn't think anything was going on. It was like I directed my own porn movie. She was a little afraid at first, but after a few humps she didn't care that I was in the room with them. "Will you have my baby?" he moaned.

"Yes, I'll have your baby, but only if you promise to take care of us."

He agreed, and exploded inside the real Tina like a rocket. And she closed her eyes covering up her face.

He wanted to take off his blindfold and handcuffs, but I told him not to because he was still my hostage. He told me how much he loved me and wanted to be with me. How this was the best sex that he has ever had, and after he'd confessed to me like a sinner at confession, the effect of the pills had started to kick in and he fell fast asleep. Tina got up and as she was putting her skirt back on, she fell and we both burst out laughing. I whispered into his ear that I would be back, and I had Tina to go back downstairs to her hiding spot until the cab came. After twenty minutes or so, when I went back upstairs, and he was knocked out cold, snoring like a pig. Tina went home without me because I had to stay. After she left, I jumped into the Jacuzzi and found a set of his silk pajamas to put on. I let him out of the handcuffs and with all my might I placed on his boxers and covered him up. I called Tina to make sure that she made it home, and I watched cable until I fell asleep. I wrapped myself up in another set of sheets next to him in the bed like a cocoon. I set the alarm clock on his night- stand for seven o'clock. I fell asleep watching Green Acres and woke up to breakfast in bed at seven forty nine. I had a ten o' clock class, so I had to rush home to get ready after I ate. I'm going to have lunch with Mrs. Graham tomorrow. Maybe I'm after the wrong person. If I can get her, I'll get the money. My plans are getting closer to the grand finale. Things are going to move kind of fast so prepare yourself.

Monday at Noon

Mrs. Graham and Tamara drove (in two separate vehicles) two miles for lunch at her favorite restaurant called Graham's House of Seafood. It didn't take a rocket scientist to figure out why she loved this restaurant so much. It was once a waffle house that she extended by having contractors tear down the middle wall and basically tripled the size of the place. When she had purchased the restaurant, she immediately decided to sell seafood because she just LOVED fish, and since SHE loved fish, she figured (quite surely) that EVERYONE should love fish. As it turned out, she was right because business was booming and things were going great. Another thing she felt RIGHT about was the fact that Tamara and her son—her only son—were not compatible for each other.

It wasn't that she disliked Tamara; she seemed intelligent and smart, it was just something about her that she could not figure out. At first, she thought that maybe it was the age difference or maybe she was after him for his RICHES, which was most likely. She'd seen women with that hawkish look in their eyes; the ones Michael, her precious Michael, had dated before. She wasn't stupid, and she was determined to get that point across to him before it was too late. She constantly tried to warn Michael (it was just her motherly intuition) about his new girlfriend. He talked quite frequently and openly of marriage. She expressed to her son that Tina (really Tamara) brought this eerie feeling to her every time they were around each other. She even went so far as to hire an investigator to dig deep into Tina's background, and she pulled out of the closet that her mother was a prostitute and had done time for abuse and selling her daughter to men for money. She couldn't wait to confront her with these newfound allegations.

"What do you want me to say? My mother abused me."

"My son doesn't need to be married to an ex-hooker," she said with a smirk on her face. "I don't think he knows about your past, does he?"

Tamara shook her head. "You are crazy."

"Honey, you can call it whatever you want, but Michael needs to know, don't you think?

He usually was never defiant and always agreed with his mother because he wasn't going to mess up his good thing, but he LOVED Ty, and he wasn't going to let her slip through his fingers. He explained this to his mother the other day at lunch, so she had to pull out the big guns.

'She's one of a kind, mother. I love her and she's going to be my wife and have my children one day, so if you're going to punish me because you're miserable and alone- go ahead,' and he stormed out of the restaurant and hadn't called her for two days now. That's a record.

"Mrs. Graham," she whispered. "Mrs. Graham, to Earth," said Tamara, snapping her fingers in front of her face.

"I'm sorry dear. I sometimes drift off into my own little world."

"Are we going to eat because I'm starving?" She rubbed her stomach. "You know I might be pregnant."

"Yea, that's what they all say," she said matter of factly.

They sat at her favorite table in the back room with a marvelous view outside. There were three fountains of water that had changing color lights inside of them. Some VIP customers could make reservations to have their food on the deck, but it cost a few extra dollars. The restaurant resided a few hundred feet in front of the woods. The inside was as beautiful and well designed as the view of the outside. The grass was beautifully maintained; she personally got onto her hands and knees to plant the roses in the garden. She put down the marble floors in the rest rooms. She'd personally chosen the interior theme for the restaurant all the way down to the Italian hand-stitched curtains. This place was a site to see, but yet it was affordable to everyone. It looked like a four star restaurant with the pricing of a soul food joint.

Of all of her businesses, (thirteen to be exact) this was her pride and joy. She left the day to day operations of her other businesses to Michael and her nephew, but this restaurant was different. The restaurant was her pet project, her baby, besides Michael. She singled handily picked every employee who worked in the restaurant. Her wait staff had to be attractive, yet friendly. The cooks had to have an awesome reference background check to be on her payroll. She'd had credit checks performed (without their knowledge, of course) on her cashiers. Even the cleaners were thoroughly checked out before they were hired. She wasn't a joke especially pertaining to the restaurant, and its daily functions. She stopped at the restaurant daily and checked the box for the customers' comments or complaints. If she received a complaint, she would talk to the person and get to the root of the problem. If the complaint was something that could possibly ruin her business you were out of there. Mrs. Graham had always dreamed of owning her own restaurant, but she had gotten into other projects listening to her husband.

"Good morning, Mrs. Graham. My name is Tanya, and I'll be your waitress for today. Are you ready to order, Mrs. Graham," asked the smiling waitress.

"Yes, I'm ready to order Tanya," said Tamara. "I'll have your perch fish and fries with a Coke and hold the ice please."

"Give me my usual Tanya. I've heard nothing, but good things about you."

"Thank- you Mrs. Graham! So that'll be baked catfish with an order of onion rings, large lemonade and no ice?"

"Correct sweetie."

"I'll be back shortly with your order and if you need anything, don't hesitate to let me know."

"Okay," they said in unison.

She arrived with their soft drinks, napkins and eating utensils and placed them onto the table. Mrs. Graham took a cigarette out of her wallet and lit the CANCER STICK. Tamara placed her trigger finger underneath her nostrils covering her mouth to avoid inhaling the smoke. **Smokers don't care about other people all they know is what they want. I'm glad I let go of those things. They make your breath stank and your teeth brown,** thought Tamara.

She blew the smoke out of her nose towards her. "From the look on your face is it safe to assume that the smoke is bothering you?"

"Yeah," but she didn't respond to the question because Mrs. Graham knew that Tamara had asthma. That was her way of being sarcastic towards Tamara. She took a couple more puffs releasing the smoke in Tamara's direction again. **This old bitch is trying to push my buttons,** she thought.

She placed her cigarette into the ashtray. "I'm not the one for small talk, and I brought you here for a reason," said Mrs. Graham.

Tamara uncrossed her legs, scooting her chair closer to the table.

"Not to eat lunch huh? I didn't think you did," she smiled.

She shook her head.

"Oh really, I'm not surprised mother dear."

"You're probably already aware that I disagree with you and Michael's relationship," she took a sip of her lemonade. She waved for Tanya's attention.

Tanya asked, "Yes ma'am. Is something wrong?"

"This is too sweet, and I forgot to tell you to use Sweet-and-Low in my lemonade from this day forward please."

She smiled. "Sure thing."

"Now, where was I?"

"As far as I'm concerned you're talking to a brick wall because you're tripping Mrs. Graham. Michael loves me and there's not a damn thing that you can do about it." Tamara had seen that the waitress was heading with the tray of food and drinks in their direction. "Before you start being all in your child's business, learn how to take care of yourself." Tamara gestured for her to go to the bathroom to clean her nose.

"You have something white hanging from your nose. Maybe, if you look in the mirror sometimes at yourself and CORRECT the wrong things you find first; you would see that you're no better than the rest of us."

Mrs. Graham quickly excused herself from the table and went into her private restroom. Tamara made a phone call. "Did you do it?" she asked the caller.

"Here's your order, and here's Mrs. Graham's order, her lemonade with sweet and low sugar."

"I love you too Michael," she hung up the phone.

"Thank you Tanya," she handed her a twenty dollar bill.

"You don't have to pay for your food it's on the house."

"That's your tip. Thank you for your good service Tanya."

She placed the money in her apron. "No, thank you….uh..Ms….?

"Ta.. My name is Tina."

"Let me know if you need anything."

"I'm fine. You go ahead and tend to your other customers before the wicked witch of the west comes back demanding you to feed her."

Tamara slid something out of her pocket fumbling with it underneath the table as she quickly removed Mrs. Graham's lemonade off of the table pouring whatever was in her hands into her glass stirring it with the straw.

She heard someone speaking to Mrs. Graham, and she hurried up and set the drink back onto the table. She started eating her food.

"I see the food is here."

"No, I'm eating air," she replied.

She laughed. "You are very humorous," she leaned in saying, "But you're still on the clock, and I will fire you for being sarcastic with me."

"I clocked out for lunch sweetie so you can go straight to hell." She leaned in closer and told her, "You are full of shit, Mrs. Graham. Who do you think you are, Misses Big Stuff? You liked me when I was just your worker, but when Michael and I got personal you started hating me." She placed a piece of fish into her mouth. "Are you in love with your son?"

She choked. "Are you crazy," she sniggered. "Question is, are you in love with my son?"

Mrs. Graham pinched off her bread, politely placing it into her mouth. "Here's the deal. I'll pay you say, one hundred thousand dollars to quit the job and break up with Michael and never be seen with him again." She retrieved her checkbook from her purse and proceeded to write. "Do we have a deal?"

Tamara continued eating her food. "You're food is going to get cold, and she went through all that trouble of making that good looking lemonade for you, the least thing that you could do is drink it."

She **killed** the glass of ice-cold lemonade. "Do we have a deal?"

"I'll tell you what- I'm going to have his baby with or without your permission. I was sick this morning, so I might be pregnant with Michael junior right now, as we speak. Did you know that we were planning on bringing a baby into this world soon?"

"He told me that."

"Every man should have a child to carry on his name. Don't you think so Mrs. Graham," she asked smiling.

"He doesn't need a six dollar and hour, project bimbo to trap him into marriage."

"Of course, he doesn't, but I'm not a bimbo, and I didn't come from the projects lady. I'm quite sure that he doesn't need an overbearing, selfish, jealous, demented mother, who thinks she has the answer to everything, but she really doesn't have a clue. You control his life with your money, and personally I think you're going to lose him after he hears how you tried to bribe me with money."

She laughed. "Do you think you're the first person whom I've had to pay off for them to walk away from Michael?"

"Well, I'm not impressed by a hundred thousand dollars. Our love can't be bought Mrs. Graham. You have kept us apart long enough."

"What do you mean?"

"He's not fully mine, because he's trying to please you."

"Name your price Tina," she started to feel dizzy. "It's getting hot in here," she started fanning with the menu. "Whew."

She whispered. "I quit, Mrs. Graham. I'm worth more than you could ever pay me. All this pain that you've caused me will come back and bite you on the ass ten times harder. I guarantee it."

She laughed. "Is that a threat?"

"It's a promise Mrs. Graham. My grandmother always told me that **GOD** doesn't like ugly, and right now you look like a hideous monster to me. I guess, I'll see you in hell, huh?"

Mrs. Graham responded. "I suppose so."

"I want you to keep my seat warm," she replied. "Thank you for the lunch. I'll get my things out of my locker later. Here are your keys to the office. Thank you for the opportunity Mrs. Graham and I'll see you at the wedding," she laughed as she walked towards the front door.

Was there any liquor in my lemonade? Mrs. Graham wondered. "Let me get home." Mrs. Graham staggered as she walked back to her car. Her keys fell into a puddle of muddy water. "Damn it!" She fished them out of the nasty water and opened the door. She locked the door using her elbow because she couldn't hit the electric lock button. Her head started spinning faster, she was in no shape to drive, but she figured that she could make it. She had driven home intoxicated many times before. She was going to have whoever head was responsible for messing with her drink. She put the keys into the ignition and sped off while Barry White's, "Can't get enough of your love babe" played on the car stereo.

She took a shortcut that knocked off ten minutes of travel time to get home from the restaurant. She was on Route 1B going seventy miles per hour. She bent around the curve, and as she went to put on her brakes, she discovered that they wouldn't stop. She screamed for God, as she hysterically pumped her brakes turning the wheel to avoid crashing.

"Oh God, help me," she prayed, covering her face.

She had no other choice but to swerve the car into the wall to avoid a head on collision with a vehicle that was headed in the opposite direction. The impact of the wall caused her vehicle to turn over on its side. Her head and chest struck the steering wheel several times. She felt a sharp, burning sensation in her chest. Blood started oozing from the deep cut on her cheek.

"Oh God, I'm about to die," she mumbled.

A truck driver witnessed the crash and radioed in a request for help at the scene. He tried to open up the passenger side door, but it was badly smashed. "Ma'am, can you hear me! Help is on the way! Just hang on in there!"

From afar, she heard people talking near her car. She faintly heard a man's voice yelling something about flipping the car back over.

"We can't move her," a woman's voice frantically instructed.

She heard a different male's voice this time, knocking on the window talking to her, but she was losing consciousness by the second. "Don't close your eyes! Ma'am!"

She mumbled. "I can't keep them open. I'm trying, someone please help!"

The Big Payback

Tamara strolled into the crowded Texas Mercy Hospital disguised as a white man wearing a short blonde wig; blue contact lenses, and a cream colored uniform blending in with the rest of the crew. She strapped her breasts and bottom down using ace bandages. Vondell's cousin (Kathy) worked at the hospital and Tamara convinced him to steal her badge for her. She'd worn fake buckteeth, and packed on foundation that made her look like a white person with sideburns and a moustache. Tamara had transformed herself into Thomas.

The ladies behind the front desk looked up at the obvious new employee speaking to him carrying on with their business. He spoke back with his head down walking towards his first and last patient of the day; Mrs. Graham. She swiped the card that gave her access through the metal double doors: INTENSIVE CARE UNIT the sign read. There was another station of busy nurses and a receptionist. The nurses looked up at him, but kept on talking. "Good morning," one of the nurses bellowed out without looking away from her chart.

"Morning," she said as masculine as she could.

The three nurses carried on a loud conversation with each other about the soap operas and the two receptionists at the end of the desk were on the telephone.

"I hate the smell of clinics and hospitals," she thought to herself.

She walked straight into her room without anyone paying any attention to her. "There she is- my inspiration."

She brought the chair closer to the bed and equipment for easy access. Mrs. Graham laid there unresponsive. Tubes ran from every hole that was on her body. A large Band-Aid was across her forehead to cover up her hideous, deep scar from her contact with the windshield. She was hooked up to a life support machine and a heart monitor and all the cords made her look worse. She had an IV in the back of her hand and one in her left arm.

Tamara checked around before she pulled out a needle that was filled with 20 cc's of Nempholanago (a drug that was used to restart the heart after failure but too much of it would be deadly, especially to a beating heart. It was also virtually untraceable if it was administered in small doses and injected directly into the heart. The way the drug worked was tricky but she'd spent the entire year researching the medication.

She removed the sticky pads off her chest that monitored her heart and placed them onto her chest. She released the medicine into Mrs. Graham's heart recapping the empty syringe and placed it back into her pocket. She checked around to make sure that the coast was still clear, as she carefully replaced the pads back to where they had been before.

The numbers on the heart monitor started decreasing slowly. Someone walked past the room talking loud. She rubbed Mrs. Graham's hair whispering in her ear. "You can't stop me from doing what I want to do. You might've had money, but I'm smarter than you. I told you that it wasn't over," she chuckled. "Didn't I," she kissed her on the forehead. "I'll see you in hell Jackie Graham."

She stormed out of the room towards the flight of stairs making her way to the ladies' restroom, to change her clothes and remove her disguise. She had stashed a bag of clothes inside a gift bag in the air vent in the restroom. She came out of the bathroom a woman, not Tamara but a white woman with red hair and freckles. She walked out of the hospital carrying the bag, crossed over two blocks, and hopped into the car with Vondell.

"Any change in her condition?"

She smiled. "Nope, but she's resting like a baby."

DIARY ENTRY
PART 1 of 2

Dear Diary,

It's been two months and three days since the funeral. Michael took his mother's death a whole lot better than I had expected. When the accident first happened you could tell that he was hurting badly, but he figured that she was going to pull through. She was built of stone, but even stone can be crushed to pieces. I'm not judging him because people grieve differently; some cry around people as others cry to themselves. He told me that he was dealing with it the best way possible. A few times I had seen him crying as he looked through his photo book in that room where Tina hid that night. I hate to see people suffer, but it seems as though no one cares about my suffering, plus she asked for it. One day last week, I found a picture of a baby in his secret room underneath a lot of paper. I took the picture to him questioning him about it. He told me that the picture of the baby was his best friend, Vondell's baby. One of these guys is lying to me because Vondell told me that he didn't have any children and so did Michael. I asked him 'why was this picture at the bottom of the box like it was placed there deliberately.' He hasn't had the chance to hang it up yet was his excuse. He switched the subject quickly to the baby because of guilt. As a matter of fact, I know he's lying about the picture, but I'll explain it later.

Michael wanted me to go to the hospital with him when they called and informed him that his mother had passed on. I couldn't show my face in that hospital, I told him that I was getting sick. I had helped him with the burial arrangements, which was one of the hardest things that I had to do because I didn't like her for one, I hate funeral homes second, and thirdly, I was responsible for her death. I didn't want to go to the funeral, but that would've made me look too suspicious, so I bought me a black dress and went. I didn't view her body because I kept on imagining her getting up from out of the casket chasing me. Michael sat in the back with me, and I managed to make a few tears come down for my money's sake. Last night, I had to sneak Tina into the house again because he was feeling lonely, and he wanted sex, so I had laced his drinks, tying him up again, but this time he had a whole lot of drinks in him. He's starting to drink a lot more since the death of his mother. It took some time, but everything was turned over to him, the businesses, her three homes, and the cars. I convinced him when the insurance guy came to the house to handle the necessary business to transfer the money into his account, to put me down as his beneficiary because I was going to be his wife soon. Why wait until it's too late? I told him that I didn't want to struggle with our baby, if something happened to him. I ran into the bathroom like I had to throw up. I had to rub that shit in thick to prove a point to him. He signed me as the beneficiary on everything. I've been away from home so much my babies don't cry when I leave. Well, Caylyn never cried anyway, but Jaylyn did and now he waves and continues playing. I had Tina to quit her job because I needed her home with the kids while I took care of this business, plus she was really sick from being pregnant. Michael doesn't ask me to have sex with him as much because I told him that during a previous pregnancy, I'd miscarried because I was having sex during the pregnancy, so we watched a lot of television. We always caught the latest movies and went out to dinner every night. I go with him to handle his business, so I can learn how to run my own business someday. I told Vondell that we should wait at least four months before executing the plan because that's too soon, and I would've been the first person they suspected, so he agreed with me. I knew he would because I made the plan up from the beginning.

I've got four more months of this bullshit. I'm tired of thinking and plotting all this stuff. I'm exhausted from thinking of the plans, let alone carrying the stuff out.

I'll talk at you later, Diary

The Truth Shall Set You Free

The year is 1995, the 1st day of September and Tina and Michael relaxed on a beach in Honolulu, Hawaii for their last day of vacation. She's starting to show a bulge, but little did he know that Tamara always had a belly, she just wore girdles to hide her big stomach. She slept and ate. She really didn't enjoy the vacation except for when she'd made an excuse to slip away to meet Vondell in another hotel room.

She tried talking him out of going, but he told her that he needed a vacation because his mother didn't believe in taking breaks or vacations, so off to Hawaii they went (Michael, Vondell, Tamara and some girl Vondell brought along with him.) Michael spent his time on the beach at the liquor stand checking out the women who he thought couldn't compete with his beautiful wife. It was just as a much as a surprise to her as it was to Vondell. That's why he was adamant about going to Hawaii. Vondell wasn't happy about the situation, but he had to roll with the punches. Tamara told him not to worry about a thing that was better than being just a girlfriend.

They packed and headed back to Texas. On the fifth, class was starting for Tamara. Tina visited her physician last week, and had an ultrasound performed, and she's having a baby girl and Michael's excited about it. Tina (the real Tina) is pregnant by Michael, and she had an ultrasound done and it's a girl. It took a few times, but she became pregnant after the second or third time. They have two different identifications cards making them have to go to two different dentists and clinics. They worked under their fake names but it'll all be over soon and things could go back to normal.

Tina officially found out last month that she was four months pregnant. She always wanted a baby after she miscarried because she had been raped.

This was her baby- no matter how deceptive she had been to conceive her.

Today.

September 29th, it's raining hard. The cold temperatures caused the rain to freeze making the entire city shut down their business because of the ice storm.

"This state is so weak just because you get a little ice- you people freak out and shut everything down, in Detroit…."

He laughed. "Here we go again with Detroit."

"That's right, I rep my city where I come from. Anyway, we slip and slide down the fucking streets, but we take our asses to work and make that money. We can have snow up to our knees, shit; we can have snow up to our doors- blocking us in and we'd shovel our asses out of the house, or get fired because our businesses aren't closing for shit. Jesus could come down and say to the owners, "Shut down all the businesses. Rest for five days or get punished." She said laughing, as she pushed him. "You think that they would? I could name a few businesses right off the top of my head that the owners would be defiant trying to make a dollar and would go to hell. I can hear them now saying, "Wait a minute Jesus! Just a few more hours Lord because I have to beat last year sales."

He laughed. "I don't think they would be that stupid. What company are you talking about?"

"My boyfriend worked at an oil change place some years back and the owner was money hungry like that."

The phone ranged. He quickly answered it.

She cracked the eggs into the bowl, but her attention was on his phone conversation.

He had this strange look on his face. "When?" he asked.

She heard Vondell's voice on the other end of telephone. She couldn't make out what he was saying, but whatever they talked about had Michael eyes bucked. "I'll be there as soon as I can."

She stood at the stove slowly scrambling the eggs. "What's wrong Michael?"

"Vondell told me that somebody had broken into Graham's Ketchup and had stolen the television out of the lobby with the coffee pots and had vandalized the machines and the inside of the building."

She looked shocked. "You should call the police?"

"He already did. They're on their way now."

"What made him go check on the place, and everything is closed down?"

"Vondell doesn't ever sit still. He's from Chicago, so he's used to the weather like you are. He said he drove past and seen some guys running out the building with the television."

"Do you want me to go with you?"

He kissed her on the forehead. "No baby, it's too dangerous for me to be out here driving."

"It's ten thirty in the morning, why don't you let him handle it. Isn't that what you pay him for to handle minor things like this?"

He rushed upstairs to put on his clothes. "I should've followed my first mind and put on my clothes when I got out of the shower early," he thought and said out loud to himself. He quickly gathered some clothes from the closet, quickly put them on and ran back downstairs. "I'll be back shortly baby."

"Okay," she answered. She glanced up at him, and then burst out laughing.

"What's so funny?"

She fixed his collar. "You buttoned up your shirt wrong and one of your pant legs are not down," she said, a little giddy.

"Thank you. I'll be back mama. I love you."

"You're welcome, and okay daddy, I love you too," she rolled her eyes and smiled. She watched him out of the window and as soon as he pulled off she ran to the phone. "He's on his way so give him about forty five minutes. Stick with the plan! Don't fuck this up for us and don't punk out. Don't worry about me, follow instructions baby," she hung up.

She finished making breakfast and sat at the table eating. "Today is the day. There's no turning back now, and it's not like I would do that anyway." She grabbed her suitcase from underneath her bed and unlocked it. She was married to him, but she never unpacked her suitcase and had her own separate room. The excuse she had given him was that he snored when he slept and that she liked sleeping alone.

This special suitcase contained a diary, a white T- shirt with a picture on it and a black pair of jeans, some gloves that were still packed in its plastic and a picture. She had picked out this outfit three weeks ago for this special occasion. "This is my good luck outfit," she said to herself. She had chill bumps over her body thinking about what she was about to do. She quickly threw on her LUCKY outfit and went into Michael's safe borrowing a few of his items from it and stormed out the door.

"I'll need these," she snatched the keys off of the key holder in the dining room. She placed another call. "Are you there?"

"Okay, I'll see you later," she said shaking her head out of disbelief that people could be so stupid. She placed the suitcase in the trunk and quickly backed out the garage.

She pulled into the Graham's parking lot. She knocked three times on the employee's entrance door as planned. Vondell opened the door and gave her a long, seductive tongue kiss for about a minute. "Hey baby."

"Hey my smart, handsome, strong man, where's Michael?"

He pointed. "By the machines, like we planned it."

We, she thought. You didn't plan a goddamn thing with your stupid ass. She pushed him gently. "Go ahead I want to make a grand entrance. Give me a minute. I left something in the car."

"It's almost over baby."

She asked if he had brought the money and drugs and sat them around like "SHE" had planned.

"Yes, I did exactly what you told me to do."

"Go ahead now, here I come. Let's get this over with," she said smiling.

He walked back into the room where Michael was as he begged him to untie him. Tamara used a brick to prop the door open as she ran to car. She took a deep breath and exhaled, explaining to herself why she had to complete this mission. "Operation Get Revenge, in full effect," she kneeled down and tied her shoelace.

"Why in the fuck are you doing this shit to me man?" Michael bellowed out.

"Because of me," yelled Tamara.

He turned his body around as far as the chair and rope allowed. "Tina! What are you doing baby," he asked shocked as hell. She was the last person on earth that he had expected to see stroll from behind the machine. She was all that he was thinking about (what is my poor wife going to do if he kills me?) And she was the one responsible for him being tied up. Go figure.

He instantly thought of the day that his mother told him that she'd had a bad feeling about her. She said that her skin crawled whenever she was in the same room with her. He thought that maybe one of the guys whom he had fired had come back for revenge. He wouldn't have expected

Vondell to be a back stabbing bastard, especially after thirteen years of what he thought was friendship. Vondell checked the rope to make sure that he wasn't able to wiggle free. He didn't want to be the one that messed up their chances of being rich.

He placed his gun back into his pants like he was instructed to do. Then she pulled her gun out telling Vondell to pass his weapon over to her.

"Huh," he asked.

"Give me your gun Vondell," she said aiming directly at his head. "Come on out," Tamara instructed.

He stood there dumb-founded, and Michael cackled shaking his head.

"Slowly baby, pass your damn gun to me."

He thought it would be a wise decision to pass it over to her, or risk getting his brains blew out. She quickly snatched it from him, grinning. "Thank you. Sit down in that seat right there!"

She yelled to one of her guests. "Come on and tie him up," she tossed the rope to the masked person. The men looked puzzled as they wondered who else she had caught in her web of lies. They walked from behind the machine wearing all black.

"My hands are full," she chuckled. "And he's a little tied up right now," she said laughing.

She kicked the side of Michael's chair. "Fellows, I would like for you to meet Black Man. Black Man, will you nod what up to the fellows?" The guy who stood off to the side nodded what up to the men like he was told to do. The men looked puzzled as they wondered who else she had caught in her web of lies. "Bring me three more chairs from out of that room, right there, she directed Black Man," her puppet nodded and did as he was instructed.

"Thank you darling. Now sit one of them here for me, and there for you," she said pointing next to Michael and Vondell, and the other one there. She said, "I know I owe both of you explanations so I'll start with you Vondell," she said pleasantly.

She gently rubbed his head. "I really liked you, but I met you at the wrong time baby. I needed you to set him up more than I needed you as my man. You made love to me so damn good baby," she squeezed his crotch a little harder than he'd liked. "I'm sorry that this good thing will be wasted. She licked her lips. "I enjoyed it but hey, what can I say? Money over bitches," she shrugged her shoulders spreading her hands like she was weighing her options. "Money or a man?" she guffawed, answering "Money."

She straddled across his lap and stuck the gun into his side. "Which one do you find important? Money or pussy?" she laughed psychopathically. He didn't respond. He yanked his head out of her hand. She whispered to Michael, "I can see he's a bit mad, but he should really be mad at himself for being so stupid."

He moved his legs for her to get off of him. "You're trying to make me fall huh? Okay- I'll get up because I'm anxious to talk to Mr. Graham over here anyway."

She took off her leather coat and showed him her outfit. "Do you like my shirt?"

He didn't respond at first. "You're mad too," she laughed. "Shoot Him!"

He quickly replied yes.

"Thank you," she replied. These are the twins."

"Tamara's twins," he said. "Okay."

"Yes, Tamara's twins," she smirked. "Thing is I'm Tamara."

"Who in the hell is Tamara?" asked Vondell.

"Shut him up," she told Black man and he jabbed him in the stomach with his knee.

"Now let me try it again. Yes, let me sit down right here, next to you and tell you the truth about me," she moved her chair closer to him. "Okay Mr. Graham. Here it goes, but first I need you to take care of some loose ends for me. Untie his right arm," she told Black man.

"This is for you Michael," she passed him his gun that was registered in his name, (the gun that was supposed to have been placed safely into his safe deposit box in his secret room with a six digit code.) She placed the other gun into his right temple. "Now, if you want to live you better shoot him in the head, before I shoot you!"

"I can't do it," he said sobering. She wiped his tears away using the barrel of the gun. She said frustrated.

"Why not," she asked. "He had planned on blowing your brains out without any hesitation daddy." She snatched the gun from his hand. "Punk."

"No, I wasn't man," he yelled trying to plead his case.

Tamara yelled. "Will you shut him up again but better this time?" Black Man hit him in the mouth with the handle part of the gun, and he yelled out in agony. "Man, I wasn't going to kill you," he said.

"Shut him up! He did talk too damn much." He received a mighty blow to the stomach and back of the neck from Black Man. "Shut the fuck up man!"

He pleaded once again. "Tina, don't do this shit! I'll pay you. I promise not to call the police."

She cocked the gun. "Fuck you Michael! I want everything!"

He cried out. "I'll pay you a million dollars!"

She laughed, rolling her eyes. "A million dollars, did you hear that? He's going to give me a million dollars to let him live. Do I look stupid?"

"No," he said sincerely. "Please?"

She mocked him laughing. "Please?" She played with the gun by his head. "It's a goddamn shame that it took all of this for a bitch to get paid like she deserved to. Do you know how long I've been suffering?"

He nodded sympathetically. "I know Tina. I can get you the help that you need."

She felt insulted by his comment. "Fuck you bitch, I don't need help. All I need is your money. I wanted your love, but you wouldn't give it."

"Tina, I loved you. That's why I want to get help for you."

She stood over the chair as she placed the gun into his mouth. "If you call me Tina one more time- I'll have your tongue ripped out of your mouth."

She told him to get the gun. "Last chance, before you die," she said. "What'cha going to do?"

He grabbed the gun from her. It was clear that he was nervous because he shook like a leaf on a tree. She said, "Here you need some help," he held the gun in his hand as she placed her hand over his hand. Vondell, screamed and frantically moved around trying to free himself.

The sound from the pistol was deafening as hot lead penetrated his left temple killing him instantly. Michael screamed, and Tamara snatched the gun walking away from him. "I have something to show you," she pulled a picture out of her back pocket. "Who is this?"

"I told you who that was," he yelled.

She chuckled and said exasperated, "Don't want to tell me the truth! I know who this is. You're a liar! Pinocchio- your nose is growing," she placed the gun up his nostril. I wonder how it would feel to get shot in the nose. Would the bullet go through your brain? Should I shoot you in the nose to find out? You can tell a lot about a person's feeling through expressions. Let me start from the beginning because you look lost Mickey. She pulled another picture out of her pocket. Do you know this lady?"

He looked at the picture. "Yes. Where did you find that picture?"

"I'm glad that you asked me that. These two pictures go hand and hand. You can't have one without the other. Here's my last picture that I need to show you."

"That's a picture of me and…" he stopped mid-sentence.

"Don't lie to me!" She balled up her fist and connected one to his jaw. "I've waited a long time to do that," she said rubbing her knuckles over the leather gloves. "This is you Michael and this is my mother Jeanette. This is a picture of me! You are a fucking idiot! I'm Tamara Brown and that over there in the black suit is… Do you know who the one that hasn't said a word is?"

"You're fucking crazy," he thought.

Tina took off the mask and revealed her true identity on cue like she was told. "That is Tina. Tina, say hello to Michael Trent Graham. She waved Hi to him. You two really know each other well, but you never were properly introduced." She told him, "Trent, say hello to your child's mommy, Tina Young," she said laughing hysterically. His mouth was wide open and his thoughts were going a mile a minute. He knew the possibilities of having to deal with his secret of having a love child would someday come and bite him in the ass, but never nothing like this.

He pictured his daughter being on his doorstep, but never in two million years would he imagine falling in love with his own daughter.

"Here's my birth certificate without your name on it, and my real identification card, my social security card. I have a picture of my grandma. I have you to know that it took a lot of hard work to get to you. I had to save up money and sleep with a private detective to get information on the family. Don't worry we never had sex daddy. The first few times I drugged you and lied about it, that's why you never remembered doing it. The times that I tied you up, my girl, Tina was the pony rider not I. I'm a better fuck anyway," she whispered into his ear.

"Don't do this Tamara! I'm sorry that I wasn't there for you like I should've been but-"

She shook her head. "I know old Jackie stopped you right?"

"Yes," he started crying. "I'm so sorry Tamara."

"When you turned eighteen you could've made your own decision to be in my life, but NO! You chose the money over me, so I decided that you are guilty of being the worst father in the world and your punishment is death."

"She made me choose. I wanted to be in your life."

"Is that supposed to make me feel better? That's why I took care of Grandma Jackie for the both of us. That old bitch refused to die from the car crash, so I snuck into the hospital and finished what I started. That's why I never kissed you because although I'm dysfunctional, I don't do the incest thing." She held her baby picture up to compare. "I think I still look the same. What do you think daddy?" She held the picture up to his face. "I have your pretty eyes," she batted her eyes at Tina. "What you think?" Tina smiled and shook her head.

"I have a message for you from your grandchildren." She turned around and showed him the back of her shirt it read:

THANKS 4 THE MONEY GRANDDADDY!

She stood in front of Michael, and a real tear dropped down her face. "I'll see you in hell daddy."

"He yelled out, "NO! Tamara! Don't!" She didn't but Black Man sure did, in the back of his head. She closed her eyes as the tears fell. She opened them back up and his head rested on his chest with blood covering his head and clothes. They scoffed around moving the chairs as Black Man placed the bodies the way they planned to make the crime scene to look legit. They shot the guns a couple of times to make it look like they'd had a shootout with each other. They had placed the money and the drugs in briefcases, and left. They ran towards the door. Tamara walked behind Black Man. "Shit, I forgot something," she said.

He stopped "What," he asked.

She shot Tyrese in the back of his head. "To tie up all loose ends." she laughed. Tina jumped as the shot rang out. She heard the bullet fly pass her head. Tamara shot in the direction of the other men a few times with the gun to complete the puzzle. She put the gun into his hands shooting once, so a bullet would have come from that direction. She placed some money into his pockets and business cards of the men. She retrieved his cell phone and wallet from his pocket and placed a fake identification card on him. She pulled the crack filled syringe out of her pocket quickly injecting it into his arm.

"Tamara," Tina yelled.

"Let's go Tina!"

DIARY ENTRY
Part 2 of 2

Dear Diary,

It's been two long months and I have received somewhere in the neighborhood of 5.9 million dollars after taxes along with a bunch of other fees and shit. I thought long and hard, but I had Trent buried nicely with my money. I started to have his ass cremated, but I decided against that. I'm currently trying to sell the four houses and the cars. I'm going to sell everything that belonged to them. They've succeeded, for nineteen years (minus the two that I slid my way into their lives) to erase me out of their lives, but who Am I? Tamara Brown! If I want something I'll find a way to get it. If I have to steal it, convince someone else to steal it, kill for it, convince you to kill for me- I'll get it baby! I know that I gave you the run around sometimes, but I couldn't tell you everything right then. You might think that I'm crazy for writing down the events that took place in my life. Especially stuff like this that could have me put away for a long time, shit forever. I know that you're not an actual person, but I had to let my feelings out somehow. I burn each page after I write it down so there actually isn't a diary because I'm always doing something. I know you're dying to know, "What happened? How did we get away with it?" Vondell had the place set up like Michael was shipping drugs using his business as a meeting place for dealers. Cocaine was found all over the business in his office and in his mother's office. I don't know where Vondell got the drugs from, but they were there. Five case loads of cocaine and heroin. I took Michael's two guns out of his safe deposit box. We had on gloves the entire time so our fingerprints weren't on anything. It looked as though they had shot each other over a deal that went wrong. I learned his code from one of his medicated nights I just asked him, and he told me. I figured if drugs had me signing shit, he would've told me his deepest secrets. He even confessed to me (while sedated) that he had a daughter, but he wasn't ready to meet her yet. We had the crime scene flawless. Thanks to my cop show, I've learned a lot of do's and don'ts from them. I sent Tyrese a plane ticket to come to Texas to help me execute my plan. He figured that he was helping the mother of his children, which I am not. Marion (my aunt's ex-husband is their father without a doubt), and I have always known from the moment I thought that I was pregnant. He was the one coming over to Jeanette's house when she was locked up. I was part of the reason why he was acting so strange because he knew that I was pregnant and that his marriage was going to be over if I told anyone. What I found out later was that he told Diane, and Jeanette knew from the beginning because the old nosey lady across the street was watching us the entire time, and she told Jeanette. That's what happened to their marriage, he was abusive, but he had stopped after that night they had gotten married. Diane called me some months back telling me that Marion was the one who convinced Jeanette to give the kids to them. He paid for a DNA test and it came back a perfect match. Just as they both thought. He was the father and after that they separated Diane kept my kids but he was the one who provided for them. I never planned on being the reason for them breaking up and she assured me that she's not mad at me because he was the adult in the situation, but I still feel bad for them. Not for my kids though. Damarcus and I had actually planned this whole thing together. He wasn't expecting the hot grease, but I was going to later explain that I had to do it. He knew that I was going to call grandma and that they were going to come and kick his ass, but he did it all for LOVE. He didn't plan on hitting his head, but SHIT HAPPENS! He was the one who told me who my real daddy was before grandma even mentioned it to me. He also told me that Trent had a lot of money because of his mother. I was the brain behind the operation, but I needed help so he agreed to help me. Damarcus and I had planned on being together that's what sparked the whole plan. Really, "HE" planned on being together, although the outcome would've been the same but with him and not Tyrese.

I liked him a lot, more than he'll ever know, but I couldn't split my money with him. That's why he had to go.

The insurance guy came to the house about six weeks later and gave me a check for 5.9 million dollars. Of course, they had to investigate the situation before they paid up, but everything was everything. Tina went to the bank and deposited the check, and then she transferred four point nine million dollars into my account, and she keep one million in her account for her and my baby sister. She won't have to go through all this hardship like I did to get help from his ass because her big sister already took care of that for her. I learned from the way that I treated my first sister not to treat this one like that. I will try to be a better person from now on. I'll try! Can't make you any promises. I told you that I was going to be rich. I had nothing but time to plan everything out to perfection while I was in The Loving Center.

"Why do you put so much trust into Tina? I thought that you didn't trust people? What if she betrays you, then what," questions that I ask myself daily. I have her wrapped around my fingers like I have my men. She never had anyone look out for her like I do. Her father left and her mother beat her until she wanted to kill herself. I took her underneath my wings and took care of her when she had given up on herself. What I taught her was how to survive BECAUSE LOVE IS OVERRATED! Work for what you want and being Loyal goes a long way.

A little memo to the fathers- get to know your child no matter how much money you have because your child might be a little ***DYSFUNCTIONAL*** and Tamara might be her inspiration. I don't think you would want that would you? Time is priceless.

I'll write to you later.

TAMARA LASHA BROWN

THE END!
THE END!

DYSFUNCTIONAL

LaVergne, TN USA
20 October 2010
201638LV00002B/7/P